C. W. Robbins

Practical English Grammar Made Easy

C. W. Robbins

Practical English Grammar Made Easy

ISBN/EAN: 9783337390020

Printed in Europe, USA, Canada, Australia, Japan

Cover: Foto ©Andreas Hilbeck / pixelio.de

More available books at **www.hansebooks.com**

Practical English Grammar

MADE EASY.

FOR THE USE OF

Business Colleges, Private and Public Schools and Private Students.

A WORK ON ENGLISH GRAMMAR, CONTAINING THE ANALYSIS OF MANY
SENTENCES NOT GIVEN IN OTHER WORKS, ALSO A VALUABLE
COLLECTION OF THE OPINIONS OF DIFFERENT STAND-
ARD AUTHORS REGARDING DIFFICULT SEN-
TENCES, WORDS, AND EXPRESSIONS.

PREFACE.

It is the aim of this revision to simplify the subject of English Grammar as much as possible by omitting expressions and technicalities, that in the judgment of the author are not necessary to a clear understanding of the proper use of the ' English language.

Many excellent works on this subject are now published, but the time required in which to get a thorough knowledge of them, seems to be so long that the average pupil finds himself lost in a cloud of definitions and, to him, almost meaning-less expressions, and, after completing the subject in school, he often makes more mistakes than he did before studying grammar. Indeed this sub-ject seems so hard to gain a practical knowledge of, that men of culture and ability have contended that it did as much harm in our schools as it did good.

The thoughtful teacher and student will find in this work many sentences, both easy and difficult, analyzed and explained, also many sentences and expressions that other authors have been silent on, fully discussed ; also the opinions of standard authors are given on points on which authorities seem to differ, that the teacher and student may find it a valuable book of reference, as well as a time and labor-saving text-book for school or private use.

Many exercises are given that will require the pupil to bring into use the various forms of the different parts of speech, thus giving him a knowledge of the *use* of the English language, as well as a knowledge of its theory.

ENGLISH GRAMMAR.

English Grammar is the science which teaches us how to speak and write the English Language according to that usage established by our best writers and speakers.

A Sentence is a group of words making complete sense.

The principal parts of a sentence are the *Subject* and the *Predicate*.

The Subject is that of which something is said: as, The *lilies* bloom. *Prof. J. M. Greenwood* is the efficient Superintendent of the Public Schools of Kansas City, Mo. The *trees* look beautiful. *Jefferson* and *Adams* died on the same day. The *Science* of grammar is quite difficult. How strange are his *ways!*

The Predicate is that which is said of the subject: as, The lilies *bloom*. Jefferson and Adams *died* on the same day. He *built* a handsome brick house. You can *buy* a lead pencil for a nickel. Words *give* wings to thoughts.

EXERCISES.

Analyze the following sentences:

1. Horses run.

{ Horses
{ run

This is a sentence in which " horses " is the subject and " run " is the predicate.

2. Boys play.	9. Ice melts.
3. Birds fly.	10. Men sin.
4. Frogs jump.	11. Wheels turn.
5. Children study.	12. Armies march.
6. People talk.	13. Parrots talk.
7. Dogs growl.	14. Stars shine.
8. Trees grow.	15. Rain falls.

16. Boys laugh.

NOUNS AND PRONOUNS.

A *noun* or *pronoun* may be used as the subject of a sentence.

A **Noun** is a name: as, Lillie, boy, Sedalia, and fence.

A **Proper Noun** is a particular name; as, Charles, Quincy, and Sallie. All others are common nouns.

A **Pronoun** is a word which stands for a noun; as, I, you, it, he, she, and who.

SINGULAR PRONOUNS.

Subjective Forms, I, you, it, he, she, who.
Possessive   "   My, your, its, his, her, whose.
Objective   "   Me, you, it, him, her, whom.

PLURAL PRONOUNS.

Subjective Forms, We, you, they, who.
Possessive   "   Our, your, their, whose.
Objective   "   Us, you, them, whom.

Singular Pronouns represent but one. Plural Pronouns represent more than one.

When a pronoun is used as the subject of a sentence, it should always have the subjective form.

Analyze the following sentences, correcting those that need it:

1. Her came.

{ Her (She) came.

" Her " is a pronoun the subject of the verb " came ; " therefore it should have the subjective form, " she," instead of the objective form, *her*. "Came " is the predicate.

2. They ran. 3. Him went. 4. It sings. 5. Them talk. 6. Us walk. 7. Who staid? 8. She plays.

The *Predicates* of the preceding sentences are *Verbs*.

A VERB

Is a word used with a subject to form a statement, a question or a command.*

The following words are **Verbs**:

Are, run, walk, go, and play.

Find the *Nouns*, *Pronouns*, and *Verbs* in the following sentences, and arrange according to model:

1. We walked slowly by his house, and saw the beautiful trees around it.

Nouns.	Pronouns.	Verbs.
house	, We	walked
trees	his	saw
	it	

* A *verb* is used to express action, being or state; as, He *writes;* I *am;* the book *lies* on the table.

2. Cranberries grow in this marsh.

3. The city stood on a hill.

4. Life bears us on like the stream of a mighty river.

5. Jacob loved all his sons, but he loved Joseph the best.

6. There is often more happiness in the cottage of the peasant than in the palace of the king.

7. Where did you see him?

8. I think I saw her and him this morning.

9. I think that is his book.

10. The matin songs of the birds fill the air with music.

11. The trees look beautiful this spring.

12. My head feels heavy to-night.

13. He broke our jar.

14. We saw his house.

15. Great men inspire us.

16. The boy gave his sister an apple and a pear.

17. We saw your friends yesterday.

Sentences Containing Modifiers.

To Modify means to change or limit.

A **Modifier** is one or more words used to change or affect the meaning of another word or words.

EXERCISES.

Analyze the following sentences, making corrections when necessary:

1. The black horse ran swiftly.

$$\left[\begin{array}{l} \text{horse} \begin{cases} \text{The} \\ \text{black} \end{cases} \\ \text{ran} \mid \text{swiftly.} \end{array}\right.$$

This is a sentence, in which " horse " is the subject, and " ran " is the predicate. The subject " horse " is

modified by " the " and " black," the predicate " ran,"
is modified by " swiftly."

2. The man labors.
3. Us go slowly.
4. Some fowls swim.
5. Green trees grow.
6. Large, heavy bodies move slowly.
7. The old oak grew rapidly.
8. Him swam nicely.
9. Small children sleep soundly.
10. The old man walked away very rapidly.

$$\begin{cases} \text{man} \begin{cases} \text{The} \\ \text{old} \end{cases} \\ \text{walked} \begin{cases} \text{away} \\ \text{rapidly} \mid \text{very} \end{cases} \end{cases}$$

11. He read quite slowly.
12. The man spoke very eloquently.
13. John walks very swiftly.
14. The gray horse walks slowly.
15. That tall slim boy walks sprightly.
16. The mocking bird sings sweetly.
17. The big round green ball rolls very slowly.
18. The boy rises quite early.

EXERCISES.

1. Write five common nouns. 2. Write five proper
nouns. 3. Write five singular pronouns. 4. Write five
plural pronouns. 5. Write five sentences containing
modifiers, and underscore the modifiers. 6. Write a
sentence containing a noun, a pronoun, and a verb. 7.
Write ten words that are generally used as modifying
words.

Verbs are of two kinds, complete and incomplete.

Complete Verbs make complete sense without the use of other words.

Incomplete Verbs do not make complete sense without the use of other words.

Incomplete Verbs Completed by Objects.

The **Object** is that which receives the act performed by the *subject* and expressed by the *verb*.

When a *pronoun* is used as the object of an incomplete verb, it should have the *objective form*.

EXERCISES.

Write ten sentences containing incomplete verbs completed by objects.

Analyze the following sentences, making corrections when necessary :

   1. William struck he.

      ⌠ William
      ⌡ struck | he (him).

This is a sentence in which " William " is the subject; " struck " is the predicate. " He " is a pronoun used as the object; therefore it should have the objective form, *him*.

   2. Fulton invented the steamboat.

   3. Harry saw the sun.

   4. Children study grammar.

   5. We saw him.

   6. Lillie saw you.

   7. He caught the horse.

   8. Whom has my knife?

   9. Sallie took the pencil.

   10. Allie hid the book.

11. Mr. Brown knows us.
12. Mr. Wills and Mr. Thomas saw you and Mamie.

$$\left\lceil \begin{array}{l} \text{Mr. Wills} \\ \quad (\text{and}) \\ \text{Mr. Thomas} \\ \\ \text{saw} \begin{cases} \text{you} \\ (\text{and}) \\ \text{Mamie.} \end{cases} \end{array} \right.$$

13. Him and me saw Miss Archer.
14. James saw you and he.
15. We saw Floy and Lydia.
16. Edgar and Howard know them.
17. Mr. Crawford and I caught a nice fish.
18. The old man slowly saws the green wood.

$$\left\lceil \begin{array}{l} \text{man} \begin{cases} \text{The} \\ \text{old} \end{cases} \\ \\ \text{saws} \begin{cases} \text{slowly} \\ \text{wood} \begin{cases} \text{the} \\ \text{green} \end{cases} \end{cases} \end{array} \right.$$

19. He wrote a nice letter.
20. That wealthy banker built a fine residence.
21. The Czar has a large army.
22. John wrote a long letter.
23. Mr. Williams found a new pocketknife.
24. Alice studied her lesson.
25. Whom broke that new slate?
26. Him and me got the new rope.

Incomplete Verbs Completed by Attributes.

An **Attribute** completes the meaning of the verb by describing or explaining the subject.

Analyze the following sentences, making corrections when necessary:

1. Horses are animals.

$$\left\{ \begin{array}{l} \text{Horses} \\ \text{are — animals} \end{array} \right.$$

In this sentence " horses " is the subject, " are " is the predicate, and " animals " is the attribute.

Attributes may be *Nouns*, *Pronouns*, or *Adjectives*.

When the attribute is a noun or a pronoun, the attribute explains the subject. When the attribute is an adjective, the attribute describes the subject.

The verbs which most frequently take *Attributes*, are: am, is, was, are, and were.

If a pronoun is used as an attribute after any of the above named verbs, it should have the subjective form.

The *Infinitive* forms of these verbs, however, take *Objective* forms of the pronoun when the subject of the infinitive is in the objective case.

2. Mary is queen.
3. Peaches are good.
4. Vinegar is sour.
5. The man is honest.
6. It was them.
7. The earth is round.
8. It was him.
9. Byron was a poet.
10. Vice is a monster.
11. It was us.
12. The horse is a beautiful animal.
13. It was her and me.
14. The box is square.
15. The animals are very wild.
16. He is sick.

17. He is a nice man.
18. Steel is very hard.

EXERCISES.

1. Write five verbs which usually take attributes. 2. Write five sentences containing attributes used to explain the subject. 3. Write five sentences containing attributes used to describe the subject. 4. Write sentences containing the following words used as attributes : he, she, we, you, they, and I. 5. Write ten sentences containing complete verbs. 6. Write five sentences containing in-incomplete verbs completed by attributes. 7. Write five sentences containing incomplete verbs completed by objects.

Verbs Composed of more than one Word.

Verbs are sometimes composed of two, three, or more words; as, The castle had been stormed.

⎰ castle | The
⎱ had been stormed.

In this sentence "castle" is the subject, and "had been stormed" is the predicate.

Analyze the following sentences, making corrections when necessary:

1. The little children were playing.
2. James is running.
3. You must go.
4. Have you called he?
5. Us can go.
6. The house was blown away.
7. They have gone.
8. The tree may have fallen.
9. James was discouraged.

10. Who did you see?
11. Who do you want?
12. Did you see he?
13. He did not go.

EXERCISES.

Find the *nouns* and *verbs* in the following sentences, and arrange according to model:

1. John made the box and went away; but May stayed with us until the storm had ceased.

Nouns.		Verbs.	
Proper.	Common.	Complete.	Incomplete.
John	box	went	made
May		stayed	
	storm	had ceased	

2. He must have gone before you arrived.
3. It was we that you saw.
4. Maggie and Allie study grammar.
5. Mr. Davis attended school during the winter of 1890.
6. The candy is too sweet.
7. We silently gazed on the face of the dead.
8. Industry is the road to wealth.
9. The paths of glory lead but to the grave.
10. The borrower is a servant to the lender.
11. Procrastination is the thief of time.
12. No work is a disgrace; the true disgrace is idleness.
13. The lowing herd winds slowly o'er the lea.
14. The dark smoke rises in the air from the tall chimney.

AN ADJECTIVE

Is a word used to modify a noun or a pronoun.

The following words are adjectives: good, wise, the, that, and three.

Care should be taken not to use adverbs as adjectives.

EXERCISES.

Analyze the following sentences, making corrections when necessary:

1. All badly men will be punished.

$$\left\lceil \text{men} \begin{cases} \text{all} \\ \text{badly (bad)} \end{cases} \right.$$
$$\left\lfloor \text{will be punished} \right.$$

In the above sentence " man " is the subject; " will be punished " is the predicate; " badly " is used as an adjective and modifies " man," therefore should be *bad* instead of " badly."

2. All men are mortal.
3. Many wise men have written books.
4. Dry wood burns readily.
5. Mary is a good girl.
6. Henry wrote a nicely letter.
7. Lazy pupils have poor lessons.
8. The beautiful black horses ran very rapidly.
9. The girls have three sweet apples.

Note.—The pupil should notice that such words as *neatly, safely, badly, sweetly,* and *gayly* are adverbs, and they should not be used for their adjective forms *neat, safe, bad, sweet* and *gay.*

10. I feel badly.

11. The rose smells sweetly.
12. The city looks gayly.
13. She looks neatly.
14. This board feels smoothly.
15. The boys arrived safely.
16. This apple tastes sweetly.
17. The children feel finely.
18. The young lady looks prettily.

AN ADVERB

Is a word used to modify a verb, an adjective, or another adverb.

The following words are adverbs : very, wisely, sweetly, and swiftly.

Care should be taken not to use adjectives as adverbs.

Analyze the following sentences, making corrections when necessary:

1. She dresses neat.

$$\begin{cases} \text{She} \\ \text{dresses} \mid \text{neat (neatly)} \end{cases}$$

In the above sentence " neat " is used as an adverb to modify the predicate, " dresses;" therefore it should be neatly.

2. He fell suddenly.
3. Our pupils write nice.
4. The ships sail slow.
5. The small man ran swift.
6. Are you not mistaken? '
7. The birds sing sweetly.
8. He came quick.
9. Him and me did not have it.

Find the *nouns, pronouns, verbs, adjectives*, and *adverbs* in the following sentences, and arrange according to model:

1. We silently gazed on the face of the dead. As we bitterly thought of the morrow.

Nouns.	Pronouns.	Verbs.	Adj.	Adv.
face	We	gazed	the	silently
dead	we	thought	the	bitterly
morrow			the	

2. The morning stars sung together, and all the sons of God shouted for joy.

3. He was a ready orator, an elegant poet, a skillful gardener, an excellent cook, and a most contemptible sovereign.

4. Some persons are happy while others are miserable.

5. The relations between man and man cease not with life.

6. The dead leave behind them their memory, their example, and the effects of their actions.

7. The world, with its thousand interests and occupations, is a great school.

8. The Golden Rule contains the very life and soul of politeness.

9. The oceans, the mountains, the clouds, the heavens, the stars, the rising and setting sun, all overflow with beauty.

10. The woods, the wilds, and the waters respond to savage intelligence.

A PREPOSITION

Is a word used to connect words and show the relation between them.

Prepositions taken with their objects are used as modifiers.

The following words are used as prepositions: of, by, over, for, with, at, in, and from.

A Pronoun used as the object of a preposition should have the objective form.

EXERCISES.

Analyze the following sentences, making corrections when necessary:

1. William rode from town.

$$\left\{ \begin{array}{l} \text{William} \\ \text{rode | from town} \end{array} \right.$$

In the above sentence "William" is the subject, and "rode" is the predicate. The predicate is modified by "from town." "From" is a preposition, having "town" for its object.

2. James went to town.
3. The man came from France.
4. The house stands on the hill.
5. John lives in the city.
6. They went with me.
7. The boys jumped from the fence.
8. I went by he.
9. She is loved by all.
10. The ducks flew from the pond.
11. He ran over the carpet.

12. The boy fell over a chair into a tub of water.

$$\left[\begin{array}{l} \text{boy} \mid \text{The} \\ \text{fell} \left\{\begin{array}{l} \text{over chair} \mid \text{a} \\ \text{into tub} \left\{\begin{array}{l} \text{a} \\ \text{of water.} \end{array}\right. \end{array}\right. \end{array}\right.$$

13. With who did you come?

$$\left[\begin{array}{l} \text{you} \\ \text{did come} \mid \text{With who (whom)} \end{array}\right.$$

In the twelfth and thirteenth sentences " over, into, of, and with'" are prepositions, having the words following them for their objects.

14. Who did you speak to?

15. By who was he struck?

16. With who did he live?

17. For who did you ask?

18. The man with the gray coat fell from the top of the wall.

19. With patience you may succeed.

20. Will you go with me into the garden?

EXERCISES.

1. Write ten words commonly used as adjectives. 2. Write ten words commonly used as adverbs. 3. Write ten words commonly used as prepositions. 4. Write sentences containing the following verbs used with adjective attributes: feel, looks, smells, seems, appears. 5. Write five sentences containing adjectives, and underscore the adjectives. 6. Write five sentences containing adverbs, and underscore the adverbs. 7. Write five sentences containing prepositions, and underscore the prepositions. 8. Write sentences containing the following words used as objects of prepositions: whom, me, him, her, and it.

CONJUNCTIONS

Connect words and sentences.

Such words as *and, but, or,* and *if* are conjunctions.

EXERCISES.

Analyze the following sentences, making corrections when necessary :

1. George may go, but you and me must stay.

$$\left[\begin{array}{l} \left\{ \begin{array}{l} \text{George} \\ \text{may go} \end{array} \right. \\[1em] (\,\text{but}\,) \\[1em] \left\{ \begin{array}{l} \text{you} \\ (\,\text{and}\,) \\ \text{me}\;(\,\text{I}\,) \\ \text{must stay} \end{array} \right. \end{array} \right.$$

The above is two sentences, connected by the conjunction " but." In the second sentence, " you and me " is used as the subject, therefore, " me " should have the subjective form, I.

2. John Jones sells books, and Henry Smith plows corn.

3. Gertie studies music, and James practices penmanship.

4. Mr. Park went with I, and Mr. Chancellor went with Mr. Williams.

5. You keep company with good men and you will increase the number.

6. Charles went to town, but Emma stayed at home.

7. Mr. Harness lives at Montrose, and Mr. Bosier lives at Fayette.

8. Cæsar was a general, and Columbus was a discoverer.

9. Him and John came to school, and I stayed at home.

10. They went to town with he and she, but they did not find the doctor.

11. Maggie wrote a letter, and Allie studied her grammar.

12. Talent is something, but tact is everything.

13. Mr. Smith edits a paper and Dr. Hunter practices medicine.

INTERJECTIONS

Are independent words; they have no grammatical connection with any other words. Such words as, Hurrah, O, O, Alas, Ah, and Pshaw, are interjections.

In analyzing sentences which contain interjections the pupil will observe that interjections do not modify any of the words in the sentence, nor are they modified by any of the words of the sentence.

For example, " Pshaw! I do not care."

In this sentence, " I " is the subject, " do care " is the predicate, and " not " is an adverb modifying " do care." " Pshaw " is an interjection and is not related to any of the other words grammatically.

PARTS OF SPEECH.

The words of our language are, according to *use*, divided into *eight classes* called *parts of speech*.

They are the *noun*, the *pronoun*, the *verb*, the *adjective*, the *adverb*, the *preposition*, the *conjunction*, and the *interjection*.

These " parts of speech " properly combined make up the *phrases*, *clauses*, and *sentences* of which our language is composed.

We have learned that a **Sentence** is a group of words including a *subject* and a *predicate*, and *making complete sense;* as, The man runs swiftly.

A **Clause** is a group of words including a *subject* and a *predicate*, but *not making complete sense;* as, I know now *why you deceived me.*

A **Phrase** is a group of words *having a meaning*, but *not including* a *subject* and a *predicate;* as, He is the king *of Persia.*

EXERCISES.

1. Write five words commonly used as conjunctions.
2. Write five words commonly used as interjections. 3. Write a sentence containing two words connected by a conjunction. 4. Write two sentences connected by a conjunction. 5. Write five sentences that contain no clauses. 6. Write five sentences containing clauses, and underscore the clauses. 7. Write five sentences containing phrases, and underscore the phrases.

EXERCISES.

Find the parts of speech in the following sentences, and arrange according to model:

1. Maud Muller on a summer's day
Raked the meadow sweet with hay.
Beneath her torn hat glowed the wealth
Of simple beauty and rustic health.

Nouns.	Pron.	Verbs.	Adj.	Adv.	Prep.	Conj.	Interj.
Maud Muller	her	raked	a		on	and	
summer's		glowed	the		with		
day			sweet		beneath		
meadow			torn		of		
hay			the				
hat			simple				
wealth			rustic				
beauty							
health							

2. Charles gave a ripe peach to the sick woman.

3. Hamilton smote the rock of national resources, and abundant streams of revenue burst forth.

4. Put not your trust in money, but put your money in trust.

5. We Americans are all cuckoos, for we build our homes in the nests of other birds.

6. Who gave you those beautiful flowers?

7. Socrates was one of the greatest sages the world ever saw.

8. The Arabian Empire stretched from the Atlantic to the Chinese Wall, and from the shores of the Caspian Sea to those of the Indian Ocean.

9. Tell me not in mournful numbers.
   Life is but an empty dream.

10. I bring fresh showers for the thirsty flowers,
    From the sea and the stream.

11. Honor and shame from no condition rise;
    Act well your part, there all the honor lies.

12. How dear to my heart are the scenes of my child-
    hood.

13. Poor wanderers of a stormy day,
    From wave to wave we're driven.

14. There brighter suns dispense serener light,
    And milder moons imparadise the night.

15. 'Tis midnight's holy hour, and silence now
    Is brooding like a gentle spirit o'er
    The still and pulseless world.

A CONJUNCTIVE PRONOUN *

Is a word used as a *conjunction* and a *pronoun* at the same time.

The following words are used as conjunctive pronouns: *who, whose, whom, which, that,* and sometimes *as.*

The conjunctive pronoun stands for some preceding noun or pronoun, and also performs the office of a *conjunction* by connecting the clause to the word for which the pronoun stands.

EXERCISES.

Analyze the following sentences, making corrections when necessary:

1. The man who sells berries is at the door.

$$\begin{bmatrix} \text{man} \begin{cases} \text{The} \\ \begin{cases} \underline{\text{who}} \\ \underline{\text{sells}} \mid \text{berries} \end{cases} \end{cases} \\ \text{is} \mid \text{at door} \mid \text{the} \end{bmatrix}$$

In the above sentence " who " is a conjunctive pronoun, the subject of the verb sells, and connects the clause " who sells berries " to " man."

2. It was I that saw you.

$$\begin{cases} \text{It} \\ \text{was} - \text{I} \end{cases} \begin{cases} \underline{\text{that}} \\ \underline{\text{saw}} \mid \text{you} \end{cases}$$

3. Mr. Smith whom is a lawyer wrote the deed.

---

* A conjunctive pronoun and a relative pronoun are one and the same thing. The pupil may use either term. We have chosen the term " conjunctive pronoun " on account of its apparent adaptability to the office which performs. The term " relative pronoun," the word however, is the one more frequently employed.

4. He who studies will excel.
5. It was *me that* took your book.
6. It is *her that* plays the organ.
7. The man who committed the act went away.
8. They who forsake the law praise the wicked.
9. The man who sung the song is a physician.
10. The doctor who cured him lives in Sedalia.
11. The clerk who copied the deed wrote rapidly.
12. The man who you saw lives in the city.

$$\left[\begin{array}{l} \text{man} \left\{ \begin{array}{l} \text{The} \\ \left[\begin{array}{l} \text{you} \\ \text{saw} \mid \text{who} \, (whom) \end{array} \right. \end{array} \right. \\ \text{lives} \mid \text{in city} \mid \text{the} \end{array} \right.$$

In the above sentence "man" is the subject, and "lives" is the predicate. The subject is modified by "the" an adjective, and by the clause "who you saw," of which "you" is the subject, "saw" is the predicate, and "who" is a conjunctive pronoun, used as the object of the verb "saw;" therefore it should have the objective form, *whom*. The predicate is modified by the phrase "in the city." "In" is a preposition, having "city," a noun, for its object. City is modified by "the," an adjective.

13. The bird which was crippled died.
14. The man who you saw is our President.
15. The house which stands on the hill belongs to me.
16. The paper which contained the notice was the Democrat.
17. He is a man who I like.
18. The dog which you struck ran away.
19. It was a horse that you saw.
20. The man with who I went has returned.
21. He that cannot ride should not keep a horse.
22. The girls who sent the apples will never forget it.

23. A man who is wise will avoid evil.

24. The greatest man is he who chooses the right with invincible resolution.

EXERCISE.

Write and diagram six sentences containing conjunctive pronouns.

A CONJUNCTIVE ADVERB

Is a conjunction and an adverb united in one word.

Some words frequently used in this manner are: *when, while, where,* and *as.*

A *Conjunctive Adverb* modifies the *verb* in the clause and connects the clause to the *verb* in the main part of the sentence.

EXERCISES.

Analyze the following sentences, making corrections when necessary:

1. John ran when Henry left.

$$\left[\begin{array}{l} \text{John} \\ \quad \text{ran} \left[\begin{array}{l} \text{Henry} \\ \text{left} \mid \textbf{when} \end{array}\right. \end{array}\right.$$

In the above sentence " John " is the subject and " ran " is the predicate. The predicate, " ran," is modified by the clause " when Henry left,"in which " Henry " is the subject and " left " is the predicate. " When " is a conjunctive adverb modifying " left," and connecting the clause " when Henry left " to " ran."

2. Bats fly when it is dark.

3. Water freezes when it is cold.

4. We live where apples grow.

5. I shall go when he arrives.

6. He defends himself when he is attacked.

7. Flowers bloom when spring returns.

8. You do as I do.

9. The people were astonished when they heard her voice.

Write and diagram six sentences containing conjunctive adverbs.

CLAUSES

May be used as *subjects*, *attributes*, or *objects*.

Do right is a good rule.

$$\left[\begin{array}{l} \left[\begin{array}{l} [\text{you}] \\ \text{Do} \mid \text{right} \end{array} \right. \\ \text{is} - \text{rule} \left\{ \begin{array}{l} \text{a} \\ \text{good} \end{array} \right. \end{array} \right.$$

In the above sentence " Do " is a verb, having its subject understood. " You do right " is a clause used as the subject of the verb " is ; " " rule " is the attribute of " is," and is modified by " a " and " good," adjectives. " Right " is a noun used as the object, of the verb " do."

His last words were, " *Remember me.*"

$$\left[\begin{array}{l} \text{words} \left\{ \begin{array}{l} \text{His} \\ \text{last} \end{array} \right. \\ \text{were} \left\{ \begin{array}{l} [\text{you}] \\ \text{Remember} \mid \text{me.} \end{array} \right. \end{array} \right.$$

" You remember me " is a clause used as the attribute of the verb " were."

I hope *you may never be sick.*

$$\left[\begin{array}{l} \text{I} \\ \text{hope} \left[\begin{array}{l} \text{you} \\ \text{may be} - \text{sick} \\ \overline{} \mid \text{never} \end{array} \right. \end{array} \right.$$

The clause " you may never be sick " is the object of

the verb " hope."   " May be " is modified by " never,'' an adverb.

EXERCISES.

1. Write and diagram five sentences containing a clause used as the subject. 2. Write and diagram six sentences containing a clause used as the attribute. 3. Write and diagram six sentences containing a clause used as the object. 4. Write a sentence containing the pronoun " myself " correctly used. 5. Write a sentence containing the pronoun " themselves " correctly used.

AN EXPLETIVE

Is a word used to introduce a sentence or a clause without having any particular relation to it.

It, *that*, and *there* are frequently used as expletives.

That the way is difficult is evident.

$$\left[\begin{array}{l} \left[\begin{array}{l} \text{(That)} \\ \text{way} \mid \text{the} \\ \text{is} - \text{difficult} \end{array} \right. \\ \text{is} - \text{evident.} \end{array} \right.$$

In the above sentence "the way is difficult" is a clause used as the subject, and " is " is the predicate. " Evident " is the attribute of the verb " is." In the clause " way " is the subject ; " is " is the predicate, and " difficult " is the attribute. " Way " is modified by " the," an adjective. " That " is an expletive.

My wish is *that you may be happy*.

$$\left[\begin{array}{l} \text{wish} \mid \text{My} \\ \text{is} - \left[\begin{array}{l} \text{(that)} \\ \text{you} \\ \text{may be} - \text{happy.} \end{array} \right. \end{array} \right.$$

" Wish " is the subject of the above sentence ; " is "

is the predicate, and "that you may be happy" is a clause used as the attribute. "That" is an expletive. "You" is the subject of the verb "may be," and "happy" is an attribute.

There are men who think *that labor is disgraceful.*

In this sentence "men" is the subject and "are" is the predicate. "Men" is modified by "who think that labor is disgraceful." "Who" is a conjunctive pronoun the subject of the verb "think." "That labor is disgraceful" is a clause used as the object of "think."

"Labor" is the subject of "is," and "disgraceful" is, an attribute. "There" and "that" are expletives.

EXERCISES.

Analyze the following sentences:

1. His wish is *that* we should come early.
2. He said *that* the work was already completed.
3. *That* the cause was just has been proven.
4. We believe *that* all bodies occupy space.
5. *There* was much grass there.
6. Gallileo taught *that* the earth revolves.
7. I know who did it.
8. I heard she went away.
9. I learned who sent the apples.
10. He said *that* we could not go.
11. I think *that* it will rain.
12. I know why you did it.

SENTENCES

Are Simple, Complex, or Compound.

A **Simple Sentence** is one that consists of one independent statement, question, or command; as, Henry went to town. What do you want? James and Anna will go to the country.

* A **Complex Sentence** is one containing one or more than one clause; as, He is the man *whom you saw.* They *sung while he danced.*

A **Compound Sentence** consists of two or more simple or complex sentences of equal rank; as, John went to see the lawyer, and James went to see his brother;

Mary left while John was gone, and Leona returned while Lydia was here.

They who were first shall be last, and they who were last shall be first.

EXERCISES.

1. Write three simple sentences. 2. Write three complex sentences, each containing two clauses. 3. Write three compound sentences, each containing three assertions. 4. Write two compound sentences, omitting the connectives. 5. Write two complex sentences, each containing three clauses. 6. Write a complex sentence containing a clause used as the subject. 7. Write a complex sentence containing a clause used as the object. 8. Write a complex sentence containing a clause used as the attribute. 9. Write a complex sentence containing a

---

* *Note.* A clause is the constituent element of a complex sentence, and whenever you have a clause in a sentence you have a complex sentence, it matters not whether the clause is used as the subject, object, attribute, or as a modifier.

clause used as a modifier. 10. Write two compound sentences, each composed of two complex sentences.

APPOSITIVES.

* When *a noun or pronoun is used to explain the meaning of a preceding noun or pronoun, it is called an appositive.*

The *Appositive* refers to the same person or thing as the *noun* or *pronoun* which is explained by it.

EXERCISES.

Analyze the following sentences:

1. Milton the poet was blind.

poet | the

{ Milton

{ was—blind

This is a sentence in which "Milton" is the subject; "was" is the predicate, and "blind" is the attribute. "Poet" is in apposition with Milton, and is modified by "the," an adjective.

2. St. Paul the Apostle was in the reign of Nero.

3. Mr. Jones the lawyer is a fine writer.

4. The skull, or cranium, protects the brain.

5. Mr. Smith the doctor is related to Mr. Brown the blacksmith.

6. My son Joseph has entered college.

7. I saw your brother, him who is a doctor.

8. Have you seen Victoria the Queen?

9. Brooklyn, a city in the United States, is noted for its churches.

10. He himself could not go.

Write and diagram five sentences containing appositives.

---

* Nouns or pronouns used after verbs not taking objects meaning the same thing as the subject, are used as attributes and not as appositives.

THE INFINITIVE

Is a form of the verb which may be used as a *noun*, an *adjective*, or an *adverb*. It may generally be known by " to " placed before it.

EXERCISES.

Analyze the following sentences containing infinitives:

To love is to obey.

$\left\{\begin{array}{l}\text{To love}\\ \text{is} - \text{to obey.}\end{array}\right.$

In the above sentence " to love " is an infinitive used as the subject; " is " is the predicate and " to obey " is an infinitive used as the attribute.

To be good is to enjoy life.

$\left\{\begin{array}{l}\text{To be—good}\\ \text{is—to enjoy} \mid \text{life}\end{array}\right.$

In this sentence " to be good " is the subject, " is " is the predicate, and " to enjoy life " is the attribute; " good " is an adjective used as an attribute after the infinitive " to be, "and " life " is a noun used as the object of the infinitive " to enjoy."

They wish to go to the city.

$\left\{\begin{array}{l}\text{They}\\ \text{wish} \mid \text{to go} \mid \text{to city} \mid \text{the}\end{array}\right.$

In the above sentence " they " is the subject; " wish " is the predicate.

" To go to the city " is the object of wish. " To go " is an infinitive, modified by " to the city; " " to " is a preposition having " city,"a noun, for its object; " the " is an adjective modifying " city."

To destroy a man's prospects is to blight a man's hopes.

$$\left[\begin{array}{l} \text{To destroy} \mid \text{prospects} \left\{ \begin{array}{l} \text{a} \\ \text{man's} \end{array} \right. \\ \\ \text{is—to blight} \mid \text{hopes} \left\{ \begin{array}{l} \text{a} \\ \text{man's} \end{array} \right. \end{array} \right.$$

In the above sentence " to destroy a man's prospects " is the subject; " is " is the predicate, and " to blight a man's hopes " is the attribute. " To destroy " is an infinitive, having " prospects " for its object, and " hopes" is the object of the infinitive " to blight."

1. Children love to play.
2. To err is human, to forgive is divine.
3. To be industrious is to be successful.
4. To write nicely is a useful accomplishment.
5. We came to recite our lesson.
6. The boys stopped to play by the way.
7. The child was afraid to go alone.
8. To bear our fate is to conquer it.
9. We desire to be loved by our friends.
10. To save is to earn.
11. To run is cowardly.
12. He returned to make an apology.

EXERCISES.

1. Write three sentences containing an infinitive used as the subject. 2. Write three sentences containing an infinitive used as the attribute. 3. Write three sentences containing an infinitive used as a modifier. 4. Write three sentences using infinitive phrases to modify the predicates. 5. Write three sentences using prepositional phrases to modify the subjects. 6. Write three sentences using prepositional phrases to modify the predicates. 7. Write two sentences using clauses to modify the subjects. 8. Write three sentences using clauses to

modify the objects. 9. Write two sentences using
clauses to modify the objects of prepositions. 10.
Write three compound sentences, and contract them into
equivalent complex sentences. 11. Write two simple
. sentences each containing two subjects and expand them
into equivalent compound sentences. 12. Write two
complex sentences, and contract the clauses into equivalent infinitive phrases.

A PARTICIPLE

Is a variation of the verb, which may be used as an
adjective or a *noun*.

When a *participle* is used as a noun it may be modified
as either a *noun* or a *verb* or as *both* at the same time.

EXERCISES.

Analyze the following sentences containing participles:

A man resting by the roadside found a purse.

$$\begin{cases} \text{man} & \begin{cases} \text{A} \\ \text{resting} \mid \text{by roadside} \mid \text{the} \end{cases} \\ \text{found} \mid \text{purse} \mid \text{a} \end{cases}$$

In the above sentence " man " is the subject, " found "
is the predicate and " purse " is the object; the object
is modified by " a," an adjective; the subject is modified
by " a," an adjective, and " resting by the roadside; "
" resting " is a participle modified by " by the roadside; " " by " is a preposition having " roadside " for its
object ; " roadside " is modified by " the," an adjective.

The good King betrayed by his enemies fled to his castle.

$$\begin{cases} \text{king} & \begin{cases} \text{The} \\ \text{good} \\ \text{betrayed} \mid \text{by enemies} \mid \text{his} \end{cases} \\ \text{fled} \mid \text{to castle} \mid \text{his} \end{cases}$$

In the above sentence " King " is the subject ; " fled "

is the predicate; " King " is modified by " the " and " good," adjectives, also by " betrayed by his enemies." " By " is a *preposition* having " enemies " for its object ; " enemies " is modified by " his ; " the predicate by " to his castle ; " " to " is a preposition having " castle " for its object, " castle " is modified by " his."

Being innocent of the crime, be firm and confident.

  ⌈ (you) | Being—innocent | of crime | the
  ⌊ be — firm and confident

In the above sentence " you " understood is the subject modified by " being innocent of the crime," " be " is the predicate, " firm and confident," are adjectives used as the attribute.

Reading fine print tires the eyes.

  ⌈ Reading | print | fine
  | tires
  ⌊ eyes | the

In the above sentence " reading " is a participal used as the *subject*, " print " is a noun used as the *object* of " reading," " fine " is an adjective modifying " print." " Tires " is the *predicate;* " eyes " is a *noun* used as the *object* of the *verb* " tires ;" " the " is an *adjective* modifying " eyes."

Our going to the lecture will depend upon my father's giving his consent.

  ⌈   going { Our
  | { to lecture | the
  | will depend | upon giving { father's | my
  ⌊   { consent | his

In the above sentence " going " is a participle used as a noun, and is modified by " our " and " to the lecture." " My father's giving his consent " is the object of the preposition " upon." " Giving " is a participle used as a noun, having "consent" for its object, and is modified by "father's," a possessive.

Forsaken by all my friends, I took refuge in flight.

$$
\left[\begin{array}{l}
\text{I} \mid \text{Forsaken} \mid \text{by friends} \left\{\begin{array}{l}\text{all}\\\text{my}\end{array}\right. \\[1em]
\text{took} \left\{\begin{array}{l}\text{refuge}\\\text{in flight}\end{array}\right.
\end{array}\right.
$$

In the above sentence "Forsaken by all my friends" is a participial phrase modifying "I."

1. The cackling of geese saved Rome.
2. The vessel sailing on the bay has no captain.
3. Hearing and seeing, I believed.
4. He will be rewarded for studying his lesson.
5. A tree overturned by the wind lay across our path.
6. I often think of seeing him.
7. Turning suddenly, I fell down.
8. Seeing us, they went away.
9. Having money in my pocket, I was independent.
10. Reading is a very important branch of knowledge.
11. Being weary I sat down to rest.
12. The corporal was shot for deserting his regiment.
13. A word fitly spoken is like apples of gold in pictures of silver.

EXERCISES.

1. Write four sentences using participles used as nouns. 2. Write five sentences in which the subject is modified by a participial phrase. 3. Write three sentences in which the participial phrase is used as the subject. 4. Write four sentences in which the subjects are modified by appositives. 5. Write two sentences using participial phrases as objects of prepositions.

GENERAL EXERCISES.

The pupil should study the following exercise carefully, after which the teacher should require him to diagram them and give a thorough explanation of each:

1. I speak as to wise men: judge ye what I say.

$$\begin{cases} I \\ speak \end{cases} \begin{cases} I \\ [would \ speak] \end{cases} \begin{cases} to \ men \ | \ wise \\ as \end{cases}$$

$$\begin{cases} ye \\ judge \end{cases} \begin{cases} I \\ say \ | \ what \end{cases}$$

" What " is a pronoun used as the object of the verb " say."

2. I took him to be a lawyer.

$$\begin{cases} I \\ took \ | \ him \ | \ to \ be—lawyer \ | \ a \end{cases}$$

In the above sentence " him to be a lawyer " is the object of " took." " Him " is modified by " to be," an infinitive. " Lawyer " is used as the attribute of " to be."

3. Neither poverty nor riches is desirable.

$$\begin{cases} poverty \\ (Neither—nor) \\ riches \\ is—desirable \end{cases}$$

4. Wash your hands clean.

$$\begin{cases} [You] \\ Wash \ | \ hands \end{cases} \begin{cases} your \\ [to \ be]—clean. \end{cases}$$

" Clean," in this sentence, is an adjective used as the attribute of " to be " understood, and modifies " hands."

Another method:

4. Wash your hands clean.

   { [You]
     Wash | hands | your
            |+clean

" Clean " by this method, is considered a factitive and refers to " hands." " Hands " is the object of " wash." Many of our best grammarians prefer to use the term " factitive." We, however, in disposing of words of this kind, have considered them as used as attribute compliments after " to be " understood. The pupil may dispose of them by either method he chooses.

Note. A *factitive* completes the meaning of the verb, but refers to the object.

The *factitive* may be a *noun*, a *pronoun*, or an *adjective.*

If it is a noun or pronoun it is in the *objective* case.

A cross is used to indicate the factitive and a horizontal bar is used to indicate the attribute.

5. They elected him president.

   { They
     elected | him | [to be] —president.

" President " is a noun in the objective case, after the infinitive " to be." The verb " to be " takes the same case after it as before it, when both words refer to and signify the same thing. " He " is used as the object of " elected." Some grammarians prefer to dispose of " him to be president " as the direct object of " elected," while others claim the sentence should be expanded thus, in making the analysis: " They elected him for him to be president." " President " may also be considered as a factitive used after " elected." If considered a factitive, it is in the objective case, as the factitive, when a noun or pronoun, is always in the same case as the object.

6. Between Nose and Eyes a strange contest arose.
   The spectacles set them unhappily wrong;
   The point in dispute was, as all the world knows,
   To which the said spectacles ought to belong.

$$
\begin{bmatrix}
\text{contest} \begin{cases} \text{a} \\ \text{strange} \end{cases} \\
\text{arose} \mid \text{Between} \begin{cases} \text{Nose} \\ (\text{and}) \\ \text{Eyes} \end{cases}
\end{bmatrix}
$$

$$
\begin{bmatrix}
\text{spectacles} \mid \text{The} \\
\text{set} \mid \text{them}
\end{bmatrix} \\
\text{wrong} \mid \text{unhappily}
$$

$$
\begin{bmatrix}
\begin{bmatrix}
\text{spectacles} \begin{cases} \text{the} \\ \text{said} \end{cases} \\
\text{ought} \mid \text{to belong} \mid \text{To which}
\end{bmatrix} \\
\text{was} -\!\!- \text{point} \begin{cases} \text{The} \\ \text{in dispute} \end{cases} \\
\begin{bmatrix}
\text{world} \begin{cases} \text{all} \\ \text{the} \end{cases} \\
\text{knows} \mid \underline{\text{as}}
\end{bmatrix}
\end{bmatrix}
$$

" Which " is an adjective used as a noun, the object of the preposition " to." " Wrong " is an adjective used as a factitive after the verb " set " and refers to " them."

7. Both Sallie and Clara have decided to go.

$$
\begin{bmatrix}
\text{Sallie} \\
(\text{Both—and}) \\
\text{Clara} \\
\text{have decided} \mid \text{to go}
\end{bmatrix}
$$

8.   Better far
Pursue a friviolous trade by serious means,
Than a sublime art frivolously.

$$
\left[\begin{array}{l}
\text{[to] Pursue} \left\{\begin{array}{l} \text{trade} \left\{\begin{array}{l} \text{a} \\ \text{frivolous} \end{array}\right. \\ \text{by means} \mid \text{serious} \end{array}\right. \\[3em]
\text{[is] better} \left\{\begin{array}{l} \left\{\begin{array}{l} \text{(than)} \\ \text{[to pursue]} \left\{\begin{array}{l}\text{art} \left\{\begin{array}{l}\text{a}\\\text{sublime}\end{array}\right.\\\text{frivolously}\end{array}\right. \\ \text{[is—good]} \end{array}\right. \\ \text{far} \end{array}\right.
\end{array}\right.
$$

Note. Some conjunctions join things of equal rank together, while other conjunctions join things of unequal rank together.

" Than " in the above sentence joins things of unequal rank together, hence the clause placed after " better " modifies it.

The principal words used as conjunctions to join things of equal rank are: *and, also, but, yet, nor, or, either, neither, still,* and *notwithstanding.*

The principal conjunctions that are used to join things of unequal rank together are: *if, though, unless, except, that, for, as, than, because,* and *whether.*

9. He had a sound mind, a good judgment, and a lively imagination.

$$
\left[\begin{array}{l}
\text{He} \\
\text{had} \left\{\begin{array}{l} \text{mind} \left\{\begin{array}{l}\text{a}\\\text{sound}\end{array}\right. \\ \text{[and]} \\ \text{judgment} \left\{\begin{array}{l}\text{a}\\\text{good}\end{array}\right. \\ \text{(and)} \\ \text{imagination} \left\{\begin{array}{l}\text{a}\\\text{lively.}\end{array}\right. \end{array}\right.
\end{array}\right.
$$

10. He is worth more than you.

```
┌ He
│                    ┌ (than)
└ is │ worth more │ you
                     └ [are]
```

" Worth " is a preposition, having " more " for its object. " More " is an adjective, here used as a noun.

Another method:

```
┌ He
│                         ┌ (than)
└ is—worth │ [X] more │ you
                          └ [are—worth]
```

" Worth " is here disposed of as an adjective, and " more " is the object of a preposition understood.

11. The horse ran a mile.

```
┌ horse │ The
└ ran │ [X] mile │ a
```

" Mile " is the object of a preposition understood.

Note. Nouns denoting *time, distance, quantity, quality, valuation* etc., are more easily disposed of in a diagram by considering them objects of prepositions understood.

12. The post is ten feet high.

```
┌ post │ The
└ is — high │ [x] feet │ ten
```

13. It is natural to man to indulge in the illusions of hope.

```
                                  ┌ the
to indulge │ in illusions ┤ of hope

┌ It
└ is — natural │ to man
```

" To indulge in the illusions of hope " is a phrase used in apposition with " it."

14. Huzza! huzza! Long live Lord Robin.

(Huzza) (huzza)

{ Lord Robin
  live | Long

15. He comes with a careless "How d'ye do?"
And seats himself in my elbow-chair:
And my morning paper and pamphlet new
Fall forthwith under his special care,
And he wipes his glasses and clears his throat,
And, button by button, unfolds his coat.

{ { He
    comes | with How d'ye do { a
                               careless
    (And)
    Seats { himself
            in elbow-chair | my
  (And)
  { paper   } | morning
    (and)   } my
    pamphlet } | new
    Fall { forthwith
           under care { his
                        special
  (And)
  { he
    wipes | glasses | his
    (and)
    clears | throat | his
    (And)
    unfolds { coat | his
              [with] button | by button

16. Most men know what they hate, few what they love.

```
 ┌ ┌ men | Most
 │ │
 │ └ know  ┌ they
 │         └ hate | what
 │
 │ [but]
 │
 │  ┌ [men] | few
 │  │
 │  └ [know]  ┌ they
 └            └ love | what
```

17. That book is theirs.

```
┌ book | That
└ is—[book] | their(s)
```

18. He threw the stone almost over the river.

```
┌ He
│
│ threw   ┌ stone | the
│         └ over river | the
│         ――――――――――――――
          | almost
```

" Almost " is an adverb used to modify the prepositional phrase " over river."

19. He had more money than he knew what to do with.

```
┌ He                    ┌ (than)
│                       │
└ had | money | more    │ he
                        └ knew | to do | with what
```

20. I went a fishing.

```
┌ I
│
└ went | a fishing
```

In such sentences as this " a " is used as a preposition.

21. He is more than pleased.

```
┌ He
│
└ is—pleased | more than
```

" More than " is an adverbial phrase modifying " pleased."

22. A depot is a place where stores are deposited.

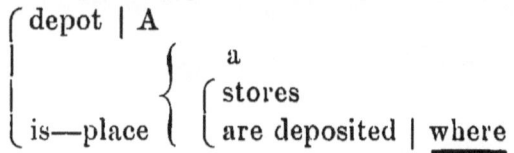

```
⎧ depot | A
⎪           ⎧ a
⎨           ⎨   ⎧ stores
⎪           ⎩   ⎩ are deposited | where
⎩ is—place
```

" Where " is a conjunctive adverb modifying " are deposited " and seems to connect the clause " where stores are deposited " to " place."

" Where " as here used is equivalent to *at which.*

23. Thus many a sad to-morrow came and went.

```
⎧ to-morrow ⎧ many a
⎪           ⎩ sad
⎪ came  ⎫
⎨ (and) ⎬ Thus
⎪ went  ⎭
⎩
```

Such expressions as, " many a," " such a," and " not a " may be disposed of as adjective phrases.

24. The house cost two thousand four hundred dollars.

```
⎧ house | The
⎩ cost | [x] dollars | two thousand four hundred
```

" Two thousand four hundred " is an adjective phrase modifying " dollars."

25. But war's a game which, were their subjects wise, Kings would not play at.

```
(But)
⎧ war
⎪            ⎧ a
⎨ is—game ⎨   ⎧ Kings            ⎧ not
⎪            ⎩   ⎩ would play ⎨   at which
⎩                                ⎪   ⎧ [if]
                                 ⎨   ⎪ subjects | their
                                 ⎩   ⎩ were—wise
```

" But " is an introductory conjunction.

26. The more I see him, the better I like him.

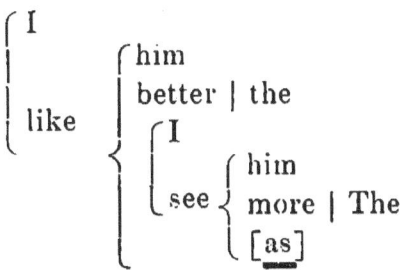

We think the simplest way to dispose of such sentences as the above, is to consider a *conjunctive adverb*
understood, hence in this sentence we have supplied
" as."

27. The shower having passed, we pursued our journey.

$$\left\{\begin{array}{l} \text{we} \\ \text{pursued} \end{array}\right. \left\{\begin{array}{l} \text{journey} \\ \text{shower} \left\{\begin{array}{l} \text{The} \\ \text{having passed} \end{array}\right. \end{array}\right.$$

" Shower." is here used independently before the
participle " having passed."

" The shower having passed " is an abridged expression modifying pursued, and is equivalent to " when the
shower had passed."

28. King David, the enemy will overcome him.

$$\left\{\begin{array}{l} \text{enemy} \mid \text{the} \\ \text{will overcome} \mid \text{him} \end{array}\right.$$
King David

" King David " is here used independently by
pleonasm.

29. Let me go.

$$\left\{\begin{array}{l} \text{[you]} \\ \text{Let} \mid \text{me} \mid \text{[to] go.} \end{array}\right.$$

Note. The sign "to" of the infinitive is omitted after the verbs *bid*, *dare*, *feel*, *hear*, *let*, *make*, *need*, *please*, *see*, and some others of similar meaning. It must be supplied in analyzing.

30. They are such as I could find.

$$\left\{\begin{array}{l} \text{They} \\ \text{are — such } \left\{\begin{array}{l} \text{I} \\ \text{could find} \mid \underline{\text{as}} \end{array}\right. \end{array}\right.$$

In this sentence " as " is a conjunctive pronoun used as the object of " could find."

Note. *As* is a conjunctive pronoun when used after the words *such*, *many*, and *same*.

31. The farm has been taken possession of.

$$\left\{\begin{array}{l} \text{farm} \mid \text{The} \\ \text{has been taken possession of} \end{array}\right.$$

In this sentence "has been taken possession of" is a verb phrase used as the predicate.

32. That man greatly lives,
    What'er his fate or fame,
    Who greatly dies.

$$\left\{\begin{array}{l} \text{man} \left\{\begin{array}{l} \text{That} \\ \left\{\begin{array}{l} \underline{\text{who}} \\ \text{dies} \mid \text{greatly} \end{array}\right. \end{array}\right. \\ \text{lives} \left\{\begin{array}{l} \text{greatly} \\ \text{[notwithstanding]} \end{array}\right. \left\{\begin{array}{l} \text{fate} \\ \quad \text{or} \quad \text{his} \\ \text{fame} \\ \text{[may be]—[thing]} \mid \text{whate'er} \end{array}\right. \end{array}\right.$$

" Notwithstanding " is a preposition having the clause following for its object.

33. Up drawbridge, grooms — what, warder, ho !
Let the portcullis fall.

(grooms)

$\left\{\begin{array}{l}\text{[you]}\\\text{[pull]}\end{array}\right.$ $\left\{\begin{array}{l}\text{up}\\\text{drawbridge | the}\end{array}\right.$

(what) (warder) (ho)

$\left\{\begin{array}{l}\text{[you]}\\\text{let | portcullis}\end{array}\right.$ $\left\{\begin{array}{l}\text{the}\\\text{[to] fall}\end{array}\right.$

34. Bird of the broad and sweeping wing,
Thy home is high in heaven,
Where the wild storms their banners fling,
And the tempest-clouds are driven.

$\Big[$ Bird | of wing $\left\{\begin{array}{l}\text{the}\\\text{broad}\\\text{(and)}\\\text{sweeping}\end{array}\right\}$

$\left[\begin{array}{l}\text{home | Thy}\\\\\text{is—high | in heaven}\end{array}\right.$ $\left[\begin{array}{l}\left\{\text{storms}\left\{\begin{array}{l}\text{the}\\\text{wide}\end{array}\right.\right.\\\underline{\text{fling}}\text{ | banners | their}\\(\text{And})\\\left\{\text{tempest - clouds | the}\right.\quad\overline{\text{where}}\\\text{are driven}\end{array}\right.$

35. Now blessings light on him that first invented sleep; it covers a man all over, thoughts and all, like a cloak.

(Now)

" Thoughts and things " are both in apposition with man.

" Like " is a preposition.

Note to Teachers. The teacher should now select a variety of exercises from different books and give them to the pupils to diagram.

We have not seen fit to put the exercises in this work as the majority of teachers prefer selecting their own sentences.

NOUNS.

A **Proper Noun** is the name of some particular person, place or thing.

A **Common Noun** is a name applied to each of a class of objects; as, *horse, boy, tree, etc.*

Nouns have *Number, Person, Gender,* and *Case.*

Number

Is that property of nouns and pronouns which shows whether one or more than one is meant.

The **Singular Number** represents but one. The **Plural Number** represents more than one.

Most *nouns* form their plurals by the addition of *s* or *es* to the singular; as, girl, *girls;* book, *books;* tax, *taxes;* etc.

Many *nouns* form their plurals variously; as, lady, *ladies;* cargo, *cargoes;* folio, *folios;* man, *men;* tooth, *teeth;* father-in-law, *fathers-in-law;* calf, *calves;* focus, *foci;* analysis, *analyses;* alumnus, *alumni;* etc.

Letters, figures, and characters are pluralized by adding 's; as, *h's, i's, 6's,* and *7's.*

When a title is prefixed to a proper name, the expression is made plural by pluralizing either the *name* or the *title,* but not *both;* as, the *Misses* Smith, or the Miss *Smiths.* When the title *Mrs.** is used, or the name is *preceded* by an *adjective* denoting *number,* the *name* is always *pluralized;* as, the Mrs. *Smiths,* the three Mr. *Browns.*

The title is always made plural when it refers to two, or more persons; as *Drs.* Scott and Brunson.

Some *nouns,* are used in the singular only; as, *gold;. wheat, music, darkness, chemistry,* and *poetry.*

News, molasses, politics, and *mathematics,* though ending like the plural, are singular.

Some *nouns* are used in the plural only; as, *ashes, billiards, clothes, bitters, scissors,* and *riches.*

Some *nouns* are alike in both numbers; as, *deer, sheep, trout, dozen, yoke* and *species.*

---

* The proper pronunciation of Mrs. is *Missis,* not *Mistress.*

4

The plural of *staff*, meaning a cane, is *staves* or *staffs*. The plural of *staff*, meaning body of officers, is *staffs*.

The word *fish* does not change its form for the plural when used collectively, but when used for individuals it is written *fishes;* as, *Fish* swim in the brook. I saw four *fishes* swimming in the brook.

Corps is alike in both numbers, but is pronounced *Kōr* in the singular and *Kōrz* in the plural. Thus: Give me a corps (*Kōr*) of soldiers. Give me three corps (*Kōrz*) of soldiers.

Some nouns have two plurals, each possessing a peculiar signification; as, brother, brothers by birth, brethren of a community or society; die, dies, stamps for coining, dice for playing; genius, geniuses, men of talent, genii, spirits; index, indexes, table of content, indices, algebraic signs; pea, peas, single ones, pease, collectively; penny, pennies, coins, pence, value or amount. In regard to " Pea," when a definite number more than one is spoken " peas " is the form used, as the pod contained four peas, but collectively the form " pease," is preferred, as a bushel of pease. The form " peas," however, is sometimes used in both senses, and when so used is by no means void of authority.

Write the plurals of the following *nouns:* money, sky, rose, potato, inch, piano, muff, sea, toothbrush, peach, solo, mosquito, cactus, gas, beau, and sofa.

Person

Is the distinction of *nouns* and *pronouns* to denote the *speaker*, the *person* or *thing* spoken to, or the *person* or *thing* spoken of. There are *three* persons: *first, second,* and *third*.

The **First Person** denotes the speaker; as, I, Darius, do make a decree.

The **Second Person** denotes the person or thing spoken to ; as, John, shut the door. Hail, Liberty.

The **Third Person** denotes the person or thing spoken of ; as, Milton was a poet. Truth is mighty.

Gender

Is the distinction of *nouns* and *pronouns* with regard to sex.

The **Masculine Gender** denotes male.

The **Feminine Gender** denotes female.

Some *nouns* such as *table*, *desk*, and *tree* have no gender. In such *nouns* as *children*, *parent*, and *bird*, the gender cannot be determined.

Gender is distinguished in *three* ways :

By a difference in the ending of words; as, count, countess; executor, executrix ; hero, heroine; emperor, empress.

By using different words: as bachelor, maid ; gander, goose : sir, madam ; wizard, witch.

By forming compound words; as, manservant, maid-servant ; landlord, landlady ; schoolboy, schoolgirl.

Such words as, *doctor*, *author*, *heir*, *poet*, *writer*, and *engraver* are applicable to either *men* or *women*.

Nouns having no gender frequently become *masculine* or *feminine* by *personification;* as, The *Sun* holds *his* fiery course in midheaven; The *Moon* shed *her* pale light on that dismal battle scene ;

Knowledge is proud that *he* has learned so much.

See how the *Ship* ploughs *her* way through the rolling waves.

Case

Denotes the use of a *noun* or *pronoun*.

The **Subjective Case** is the use of a *noun* or *pronoun* as a *subject* or an *attribute* of a verb.

The **Possessive Case** is the use of a *noun* or *pronoun* to limit a *noun*.

The **Objective Case** is the use of a *noun* or *pronoun* as the object of a *verb* or a *preposition*.

The **Independent Case** is the use of a noun or pronoun without a governing word.

The *subjective*, *objective*, and *independent* cases of nouns are alike in form.

The **Possessive Case** of nouns is formed by adding an *apostrophe* and *s* ('s) to the *subjective;* as, *Jane's* slate.

When the plural ends in s, the possessive is formed by adding an *apostrophe only;* as, *Boys'* hats.

NOTES.

1. In forming the **Possessive Case** of nouns which are alike in both numbers, the apostrophe precedes the *s* in the *singular* and follows it in the *plural;* as, The *deer's* horn was broken. A load of *deers'* horns was sold.

2. In forming the **Possessive** of proper names consisting of more than one word the sign of the possessive is annexed to the last word ; as, *John Smith's* house.

3. When two or more names are used to denote *joint ownership* of the same thing, the sign of possession is suffixed to the *last* name only ; as, *Susie*, *Pearl*, and *Lillie's* teacher.

4. When two or more nouns are used to denote *separate ownership*, the sign of possession is suffixed to *each*

noun; as, *Mr. Williams's* and *Mr. Smith's* books were lost.

5. When two or more nouns are used together and refer to the *same person* or *thing*, the sign of possession is suffixed to that which immediately precedes the noun, mentioned or understood, which is limited by the possessive; as, I bought my watch at *Townsley's* the *watchmaker* and *jeweler*.

In this sentence " Townsley's " is a noun in the possessive case, modifying " store " understood. " Watchmaker " and " jeweler " are in the possessive case by apposition with " Townsley's."

6. The **Possessive** may limit a participial noun; as, *Laura's* singing was admired by all.

7. When an intervening clause comes between the *possessive* and the thing *possessed*, the idea of possession should be denoted by a *preposition* and its *object;* as, She praised the peasant's, *as he was called*, good breeding : should be, She praised the good breeding of the peasant, as he was called.

8. In some sentences the sign is placed nearest the word possessed without regard to the true ownership ; as, The captain of the *Fulton's* wife is sick.

" Captain " is a noun in the possessive case and limits wife. " Fulton's " is a noun in the objective case, the object of the preposition " of."

9. "*Anybody else's, somebody else's*, and *nobody else's* are much better expressions than *anybody's else, somebody's else* and *nobody's else.* The latter are sanctioned by very limited authority and we would not advise the pupils to imitate them.

In the above expressions " else " is an adjective limiting the noun preceding it.

10. " *For conscience' sake*," " *For goodness' sake*,"

etc., seem to be idiomatic exceptions to the rule for forming the possessive case singular, and while they are sanctioned by good authority, it is not regarded by the best
grammarians as being in good taste to form the possessive of such words as " Thomas," " Jones," " Witness,"
" James," etc., with an apostrophe * only, but conform
to the simple rule and add an apostrophe and s ('s),
thus: " Thomas's," " Jones's," " Witness's," and
" James's."

In pronouncing words of this character the final " s "
may or may not be sounded, at the pleasure of the
speaker.

11. Usually there is no difference in meaning whether
the sign of possession is denoted by the *apostrophe* and *s*
or by a *preposition* and *its object*, but such is not always

---

* It seems to be almost a universal rule among printers
to form the possessive of such words as " Jones " and
" James " by annexing an apostrophe only; but this
method not only makes another exception to the rule of
forming the possessive singular of nouns, but in many
cases is ambiguous. For example, if there were a man
by the name of " Wilsons " and three brothers by the
name of " Wilson," and if, in the first case we should
form the possessive by annexing the apostrophe only
(Wilsons'), and if, in the second case we conform to the
rule, as we must do in such instances (forming the possessive plural of " Wilson"), we would have " Wilsons'."
Plural nouns ending in " s " form their possessive by
annexing an apostrophe only. Thus it is evident that by
this method of procedure we could not know by looking
at the name in the possessive whether three men were
meant whose names were " Wilson," or whether one man
was meant whose name was " Wilsons."

the case. There is a great deal of difference in the meaning of the expressions, "My *father's* picture," meaning a picture possessed by my father, and "A *picture of my father*," meaning a likeness of my father.

* Correct the following :

1. King James' translation of the Bible was made in the beginning of the seventeenth century.

2. A carload of sheep's wool for sale.

3. We saw Miss Minnie Jones' house.

4. Mason's and Dixon's line will long be remembered on the pages of history.

5. Napoleon and Wellington's armies deserved such commander's.

6. He attended to everybody's else business but his own.

7. You will find the books at Brown's the bookseller and stationer's.

8. They tried to prevent John going.

9. They laughed at the lawyer's, as he was called, stupidity.

10. The representatives' house assembled on the first Monday in December.

11. Men and women's shoes are made here.

12. Ladies and childrens' hair dressing a specialty.

The **Subjective Case.** A noun or pronoun used as the subject of a verb, is in the *subjective case.*

* *Note to Teacher.* If the pupils experience any difficulty in correcting the sentences in this or any other lesson, have them to diagram or analyze each sentence before attempting to make corrections.

NOTES.

1. A *noun* or *pronoun* used as the *subject* of a *verb* should always have the *subjective* form. For example:

Him who expects to succeed in life must be industrious, should be, *He* who expects to succeed in life must be industrious.

2. When a *person* or *thing* is *addressed*, that person or thing is *never* used as the *subject* of a *verb;* but is always in the *independent case* by address, thus: *John,* shut the door.

"John" is the *independent case*, and the subject of the verb "shut" is "you" understood.

3. A *noun* and the *pronoun* representing it, should not be used as the subject of the same verb; as, The *weather it* was cold, should be, The *weather* was cold.

4. The subject should not be omitted, when its omission would injure the sense.

EXERCISES.

Correct the following sentences:

1. Whom did you say did the mischief?
2. You and him will go.
3. Justice it is represented as being blind.
4. I cannot work so much as him.
5. James and me write together.
6. Him who went with me is gone.
7. Him and I study grammar.
8. Me and her went to town.
9. John and her went to the city.
10. Lillie and me are going to St. Louis.
11. You are a much greater loser than me by his death.

12. " Point out the man," said the judge, "whom you say committed the robbery. "

13. Him and his friend were almost inseparable.

14. The whole need not a physician, but them that are sick.

15. He feared that the enemy might fall upon his men, whom he saw were off their guard.

The **Independent Case** is the use of a noun or pronoun without any particular relation to other words.

NOTES.

1. A noun or pronoun may be in the **independent case** under the following circumstances:

When a direct address is made; as, *John*, shut the door.

By pleonasm,* as, *King David*, the enemy will overcome him.

When it is the attribute of an infinitive or a participle used as a noun; as, To be a good *man* is not easy. I have no recollection of his being *judge*.

When it is placed before the participle; as, The *sun* being risen, we pursued our journey.

By exclamation; as, " Oh, Popular *applause!* "

By position; as, Fewsmith's *grammar*.

---

* *Pleonasm* is the use of more words than is necessary for the complete meaning of the sentence.

In the above example if we should say, The enemy will overcome King David, the idea would be conveyed just as clearly as if we were to say King David, the enemy will overcome him.

Thus we see that " King David " in the second instance is clearly in the *independent case by pleonasm.*

2. When a pronoun is used in the *independent case* it should always have the *subjective form*, thus: *Him* having ended his discourse, the assembly dispersed. Should be, *He* having ended his discourse, the assembly dispersed.

It is plain that " he " in this sentence is in the independent case before a participle.

EXERCISES.

Correct the following sentences:

1. *Him* whom all respected, *having committed* the act, great surprise was felt.
2. Him having departed, we soon fell asleep.
3. And *them*, are not all of them going?
4. Her having gone, there was no one left.
5. Us being born in sorrow, our days are spent in misery.
6. Him being defeated, all hostilities ceased.
7. Me being young, they deceived me.
8. Oh! happy us, surrounded with so many blessings.
9. And me, what shall I do.
10. Them being absent, the cause cannot be decided.

The **Objective Case.** A noun or pronoun used as the object of a *verb* or *preposition*, is in the *objective* case.*

NOTES.

1. **Nouns** denoting *time, distance, quantity, quality, valuation*, etc., seem to be used without any governing word. They may, however, be disposed of as the *objects*

---

* The subject of an infinitive is usually in the objective case.

of *prepositions* understood, or, as in the objective case without a governing word.

The horse ran a *mile*.

This sentence is said to be equivalent to " The horse ran (*over* or *through*) a mile."

It seems very difficult in cases of this kind to supply a preposition that expresses the relation intended and in consequence of this and other reasons many of our best grammarians dispose of them as the objective used without a governing word.

2. Many verbs signifying *to ask, to teach, to give, etc.*, are apparently followed by two objects, one called the direct object and the other, by many grammarians, the indirect object. We prefer, however, to reject the term indirect object and supply a preposition to govern what many of our grammarians are pleased to call the indirect object.

He gave *me* an apple.

In this sentence "apple " is the object of " gave " and " me " is the object of the preposition " to " understood.

3. Such expressions as, *He was offered employment, He was presented a prize, He was asked a question, etc.*, are condemned by some grammarians, but as they are warranted by the best of usage, we think it much better to consider the words, *employment, prize*, and *question* as the objects of prepositions understood rather than to demand a reconstruction of the sentence upon the plea of false syntax.

4. A noun or pronoun may be the object of a *participle* derived from a verb which requires an object. Many *infinitives* also take objects.

5. A *preposition* should not be used between a *verb* and its *object*.

Correct the following sentences:

1. Who did you accompany?
2. He resolved not to permit of such conduct.
3. Who did you desire to go with you?
4. He who can learn nothing but by experience, we must surely pity.
5. He that promises much you should not trust.
6. She placed Mary and I at the head of the table.
7. I saw he whom I knew to be a rascal.
8. They left him and I on the beach.
9. The man who I saw with you is my brother.
10. He to whom much is given much will be required of.

APPOSITION.

A **Noun** or **Pronoun** used in apposition with another noun or pronoun, is in the same case.

NOTES.

1. Words in apposition must agree in case, but not necessarily in number, person, or gender; as, *They* love *each* other. "Each" in this sentence is in apposition with "they," the meaning being, *They, each,* love the other.

2. A noun may be in apposition with the whole or a part of a sentence, as "The British Parliament claimed *the right to tax the Americans without their consent,* a *principle* which the colonists opposed."

3. When *possessives* are in apposition the sign is used only with the one nearest the noun limited; as, Peter the *hermit's* eloquence.

Correct the following sentences:

1. Will you desert me, I, who has always been your friend?

2. I lost my knife near Jones', the blacksmith's.

3. Whom shall we praise? They who do their duty.

4. They are the lovely, them in whom unite youth's fleeting charms with virtue's lovely light.

5. Our Shepherd, him who is styled king of saints, will assuredly give his saints the victory.

6. Christ, and Him crucified, was the Alpha and Omega of all his addresses, the fountain and foundation of his hope and trust.

7. It poured along in most melodious energy of praise, to God, the Savior, he of ancient days.

PRONOUNS.

Pronouns have *Number*, *Gender*, *Person*, and *Case*.

Declension of Pronouns.

FIRST PERSON.

SINGULAR.	PLURAL.
Subjective, I.	Subjective, We.
Possessive, My or Mine.	Possessive, Our or Ours.
Objective, Me.	Objective, Us.

SECOND PERSON.

SINGULAR AND PLURAL.

Subjective, You.	Possessive, Your or Yours.
	Objective, You.

THIRD PERSON.

SINGULAR.

MASCULINE.	FEMININE.	
Subjective, He.	She,	it.
Possessive, His.	Her or Hers,	Its.
Objective, Him.	Her,	It.

PLURAL.

Subjective,   They.
Possessive,   Their or Theirs.
Objective,   Them.

The pronouns, *myself, yourself, himself, herself,* and *itself,* and their plurals, *ourselves, yourselves,* and *themselves,* are formed by adding *self* for the singular, and *selves* for the plural, to the possessives of *I* and *you,* and the objectives of *he, she,* and *it.*

They have no possessives and are used in either the *subjective* or *objective* cases, without change of form, thus: He, *himself,* did it. He struck *himself.*

The pronoun *it* and its compound, *itself,* have no gender.

The **Following Pronouns** do not vary their form for the different numbers and persons.

For example, "who" is written *who* when it stands for one, and *who* when it stands for more than one.

SINGULAR AND PLURAL.   SINGULAR AND PLURAL.

Subjective, Who.   Subjective, Whoever.
Possessive, Whose.   Possessive, Whosever.
Objective, Whom.   Objective, Whomever.

* *What* has no possessive and is found in the *sub-*

---

* Many grammarians consider *what* equivalent to two words ; namely, *that which* or *the thing which,* and if the teacher prefers he may so dispose of them, but *what* is simply the neuter of *who,* the antecedent being understood, just as the antecedent of *who* is understood in the sentence "I heard *who* sent it."

Mr. Butler states that in the Anglo-Saxon language the neuter gender of *hwa* (*who*) was not *hwilc* (*which*), but *whæt* (*what*).

jective and *objective* cases only ; the form being the same in each case.

What is applied to things.

CONJUNCTIVE PRONOUNS.

SINGULAR AND PLURAL.	SINGULAR AND PLURAL.
Subjective, Who.	Subjective, Which.
Possessive, Whose.	Possessive, Whose.
Objective, Whom.	Objective, Which.

SINGULAR AND PLURAL.	SINGULAR AND PLURAL.
Subjective, What.	Subjective, That.
Possessive, ——	Possessive, ——
Objective, What.	Objective, That.

That has no possessive or compound. It is used in either the *subjective* or *objective* cases.

The words used as conjunctive pronouns are: *who, which, that,* and *as.*

Who is used to represent persons.

Which is used to represent things and animals.

Whichever and *whatever* the compounds of *which* and *what* are, in most cases, used either adjectively or substantively, hence we prefer to dispose of them as adjectives or as adjectives used as nouns.

Many grammarians call *which* an interrogative pronoun when, in our judgment, it is nothing more than an adjective.

For example: *Which* will you have? The meaning of this sentence certainly is *which one* will you have. Which implies a selection and in such instances as the above always modifies a noun understood.

That is used for mixed antecedents; as, The *man* and

the *horse that* we saw. The *dog* and the *man that* were in the field.

That is also used instead of *who* or *which*

After adjectives in the superlative degree; as, he read the *best* books that could be procured.

After it used indefinitely; as, *It* was he that committed the fault.

After who used interrogatively; as, *Who* that has any sense of right would reason thus.

After the words all, very, same, etc., when followed by a restrictive * clause.

A conjunctive pronoun does not always stand for a single word. Its antecedent may be a phrase, a clause, or a sentence. His love extends FROM THE RICHEST TO THE POOREST, *which* includes all. We are told TO LOVE OUR NEIGHBORS AS OURSELVES, *which* is a christian duty. He said THAT HE WOULD NOT GO, *which* I feared. He comes WHEN HE IS WANTED, *as* is often the case. HE DID NOT COME, *which* I greatly regret. SHE SUNG FOR ME, *which* pleased me very much.

---

* When the conjunctive clause is not restrictive and could be introduced by *and he, and it, and they,* etc., *who* or *which* and not *that* are usually used.

For example: Longfellow, *that* is the most popular American poet, has written beautiful prose. In this case "that" should be *who.*

Some grammarians claim that *that* should always be used in *restrictive clauses,* but all admit that modern writers do not observe this distinction. There are many restrictive clauses, however, and especially those following some form of the pronouns *I, you, it, she,* and *he,* in which it is much more euphonious to use *that* than *who* or *which.*

Correct the following sentences and give reasons for correction:

1. All which we hope for is sometimes denied to us.

2. The traveler gave an amusing description of the persons and animals which he had seen.

3. All who knew him respected him.

4. He drives the fastest horses which can be had.

5. It was she whom you saw.

6. This is the same horse which we saw yesterday.

7. Who was it who struck you?

8. To him who hath, much shall be given.

9. He is the very man whom we want.

10. The ablest man who ever lived could not solve that problem.

11. Both the rider and the steed which we saw were killed.

12. Give sorrow words; the grief who does not speak breaks the heart.

EXERCISES.

1. Write four sentences in which " that " is correctly used instead of who. 2. Write three sentences in which " that" is used to represent mixed antecedents. 3. Write four sentences in which " that " is used as an adjective. 4. Write four sentences in which " that" is used as a conjunction. 5. Write three sentences in which " that" is used as a conjunctive pronoun. 6. Write three sentences in which " what " is used as a simple pronoun. 7. Write sentences illustrating the proper use of whoever, whosever, whomever, whichever, and whatever. 8. Write a sentence in which " that " is used to represent a singular antecedent. 9. Write a sentence in which " who " is used to represent a plural antecedent. 10. Write three sentences in which " which " is

used as an adjective. 11. Write two sentences in which " as " is used as a conjunctive pronoun.

EXERCISES FOR ANALYSIS.

1. A man who is industrious will prosper.

This is a *complex sentence*, in which " man " is the subject; " will prosper " is the predicate. The subject is modified by the adjective " a " and by the clause " who is industrious."

" Man " is a *common noun, third person, singular number, masculine gender*, in the *subjective case*, the subject of " will prosper."

" Will prosper " is a *verb*.

" Who " is a *conjunctive pronoun, third person, singular number, masculine gender, subjective case*, the subject of " is," and stands for the noun " man."

" Is " is a *verb*.

" Industrious " is an *adjective* used as an *attribute*, and modifies the pronoun " who."

2. I must not be tardy.

3. Those who sow will reap.

4. Attention is the stuff of which memory is made.

5. The sick man should be well taken care of.

6. Sugar is sweet.

7. Some, cupid kills with arrows; some with traps.

8. They are such as I could find.

9. Unless he puts a bridle on his tongue, the babbler will soon shut himself out from all society.

10. The queen seated herself on the throne which had been prepared for her.

11. Quoth the raven, " nevermore."

12. Go to the ant, thou sluggard ; consider her ways, and be wise.

13. Winter set in early.

14. Those evening bells!— how many tales their music tells.

15. Tell me, my soul, can this be death?

16. The rounded hills slope gently to the sea.

17. Judge not, and ye shall not be judged.

18. I have but one lamp by which my feet are guided, and that is the lamp of experience.

19. During the Revolution the Americans fought for independence.

20. Whoever sows shall reap.

21. Now come the soft, smoky days of delightful weather, which will soon be followed by the sharp blasts of bleak December.

22. I thought it was he that did it.

23. I took it to be them.

24. I know him to be a lawyer.

25. If I were he I should be a physician.

26. He is the man that we saw.

27. It was he that took Burton to be a preacher.

28. John wishes Mary to be queen.

29. This is Laura, she whom we all love.

30. You, yourself, told me so.

31. If I forget thee, O Jerusalem, let my right hand forget her cunning.

32. I do not care a straw.

33. Bright and joyful is the morn.

34. My opening eyes with rapture see the dawn of this returning day.

 * 35. Pope skimmed the cream of good sense and expression whenever he could find it.

----

 * If more sentences are desired the teacher may supply them from the readers or any other suitable books used in the school.

PRONOUNS

Agree with the nouns for which they stand in *gender*, *person*, and *number*.

1. To avoid the appearance of egotism, *we* is sometimes used by *authors*, *editors*, and *others* to represent a *noun* in the *singular*.

2. In the use of pronouns, the *second person* should precede the *third* and the *third* the *first*. In acknowledging a fault this is reversed.

3. A pronoun used to represent two or more nouns connected by *and* should have the *plural* form ; as *John* and *James* have lost *their* way.

4. If two or more nouns in the singular connected by *and*, are preceded by *every*, *each*, *no*, or a *similar adjective*, they are considered *separately*, and represented by a *pronoun* in the *singular;* as, *every* word and *every* thought has *its* effect upon us.

5. A pronoun which represents *two* or *more* nouns in the *singular*, connected by *or*, or *nor*, should be in the *singular;* as, Neither *John* nor *James* was aware of *his* danger.

6. If *one* of the nouns connected by *or*, or *nor*, is *plural*, the pronoun representing it should be plural, and the *plural noun* should be placed *nearest the pronoun;* as, Neither the *captain* nor his *men* were aware of *their* danger.

7. When the objects composing the unit denoted by a *collective noun* are considered *collectively*, the noun should be represented by a pronoun in the *singular* number; as, *Congress* holds *its* meetings in the capitol of the United States.

8. When the objects composing the unit denoted by a collective noun are considered *separately*, the noun should be represented by a pronoun in the *plural* number ; as, The *jury* were quarreling at the time of *their* disagreement.

9. Nouns in the singular number but of different genders connected by *or* or *nor* may be represented by a *singular* masculine pronoun ; as, The *boy* or the *girl* has lost *his* pen ; or a reconstruction may be made ; as, The *boy* has lost *his* pen or the *girl* has lost *hers*.

10. The *gender* of a pronoun representing two or more nouns of different genders, connected by *and*, cannot be determined, as, The *boy* and the *girl* lost *their* way.

11. A *conjunctive* pronoun should be placed as near as possible to the word for which it stands.

12. *Whom* and *which* should generally follow the prepositions, but precede the verbs by which they are governed.

The possessive of *which* is *whose*.

13. As there is no pronoun in the English language, which, in the singular, may represent either the *masculine* or the *feminine* gender, *usage* has sanctioned the *masculine forms;* as, The *teacher* who loves *his* pupil is interested in *his* welfare.

14. *What* is so frequently used for the conjunction *that*, by good speakers, that the usage seems to be warranted ; as, I do not know but *what* (*that*) there is truth in your statement.

15. *It* is often used *indefinitely* or to represent an antecedent understood, for example: The *ground;* as, *It is muddy;* the *weather;* as, *it is cold.*

16. *It* when used as the subject of the verb *be* is frequently followed by an *antecedent* with which *it does not agree:* as, *It is I, It is they, It is John,* etc.

17. If a pronoun in the plural is used to represent *two* or *more nouns* or *pronouns* of *different persons* connected by *and*, the pronoun should be in the *first person* if any of the words it represents is in the *first person*. If *no words* are in the *first person* the pronoun should be in the *second person* provided any of the words for which it stands is in the *second person;* as, *Mr. Williams* and *I* are going to *our* homes. *You* and *he* failed in *your* efforts.

18. The adjectives *each, one, either* and *neither*, are always in the *third person singular;* and, when they are the principal words in their clauses they require the *verbs* and *pronouns* to agree with them ; as, *Each* of you *is* entitled to *his* part.

EXERCISES.

Correct the following sentences and give reasons for corrections:

1. Let every boy answer for themselves.

2. Neither Nelson nor the officers under his command failed to do all in his power to defeat the enemy.

3. The committee, every member being present, differed in its opinion respecting the justice of the proposed law.

4. Both James and Samuel learned his lesson.

5. They had some victuals left and we ate it.

6. You and your friends cannot always have their wishes gratified.

7. A teacher should always consult the interests of her pupils.

8. You and I must be diligent in your studies.

9. The task was too difficult for the boy which had been assigned to the class.

10. Everyone in the family should know their duty.

11. He should not keep a horse that cannot ride.

12. And nobody else would make that city their refuge any more.

13. He instructed and fed the crowds who surrounded him.

14. Every man is entitled to liberty of conscience, and freedom of opinion, if he does not pervert it to the injury of others.

15. They need no spectacles that are blind.

16. The news came of defeat, but no one believed them.

17. Everyone should have their lives insured.

18. Neither the teacher nor the scholars used his books in the class.

VERBS

Have five forms as follows : *Sing, sings, sang, sung*, and *singing*.

The *principal parts* of the verb are: The *present tense*, the *past tense*, and the *perfect participle*.

Verbs which form their past tense and perfect participles by the addition of *ed* to the present tense, are *regular verbs*, all others are *irregular verbs*.

The Principal Parts of the Verb.

PRESENT TENSE.	PAST TENSE.	PERFECT PARTICIPLE.
I see,	I saw,	I have seen,
They call,	They called,	They have called,
I go,	I went,	I have gone,
They run,	They ran,	They have run,
I come,	I came,	I have come,
I write,	I wrote,	I have written.

Verbs vary their forms to agree with the different persons and numbers of their subjects.

Forms of the Verb.

I am,	We are,
I was,	We were,
He is,	They are,
He has,	They have,
He writes,	They write,
He runs,	They run,
He goes,	They go,
She sings,	They sing.

Care should be taken to use the correct form of the verb. The following sentences are correct; notice the forms of the verbs:

1. The horse runs. 2. The horses run. 3. The bird flies. 4. The birds fly. 5. He loves to sing. 6. They love to sing. 7. The girl studies. 8. The girls study. 9. I am going. 10. They are going. 11. The man writes. 12. The men write.

The following sentences have incorrect forms of the verb, correct them:

1. James talk. 2. They loves. 3. He drink. 4. They goes. 5. He have ridden. 6. They has ridden. 7. He wear a silk hat. 8. They writes beautiful letters.

DEFECTIVE VERBS.

A verb which has not *three* principal parts is said to be *defective*. The following are defective verbs:

PRESENT TENSE.	PAST TENSE.
Beware,	————
Can,	Could,
May,	Might,
Must,	————
Ought,	Ought,
Shall,	Should,
Will,	Would.

Auxiliary Verbs are used in the formation of other verbs. The words used as such are: be, do, have, can, may, shall, will, must, and need.

Can, *may*, *must*, *shall*, and *will* are used as auxiliary verbs only.

TENSES

Are variations of the verb which distinguish difference in time.

The **Present Tense** denotes present time.

The **Past Tense** denotes past time.

The **Future Tense** denotes future time.

We give below the principal parts of some of the most important of the irregular verbs:

PRESENT.	PAST.	PERFECT PARTICIPLE.
Be or am,	Was,	Been,
Be	Began,	Begun,
Blow,	Blew,	Blown,
Break,	Broke,	Broken,
Choose,	Chose,	Chosen,
Come,	Came,	Come,
Do,	Did,	Done,
Draw,	Drew,	Drawn,
Drink,	Drank,	Drunk,
Drive,	Drove,	Driven,
Eat,	Ate,	Eaten,
Fall,	Fell,	Fallen,
Fly,	Flew,	Flown,
Freeze,	Froze,	Frozen,
Go,	Went,	Gone,
Get,	Got,	Got,
Give,	Gave,	Given,
Grow,	Grew,	Grown,
Have,	Had,	Had,

PRESENT.	PAST.	PERFECT PARTICIPLE.
Know,	Knew,	Known,
Lay,	Laid,	Laid,
Lie (to rest),	Lay,	Lain,
Ride,	Rode,	Ridden,
Ring,	Rang or rung,	Rung,
Rise,	Rose,	Risen,
Run,	Ran,	Run,
See,	Saw,	Seen,
Set,	Set,	Set,
Sit,	Sat,	Sat,
Shake,	Shook,	Shaken,
Sing,	Sang or Sung,	Sung,
Slay,	Slew,	Slain,
Speak,	Spoke,	Spoken,
Steal,	Stole,	Stolen,
Swim,	Swum or Swam,	Swum,
Take,	Took,	Taken,
Tear,	Tore,	Torn,
Throw,	Threw,	Thrown,
Wear,	Wore,	Worn,
Write,	Wrote,	Written.

SHALL AND WILL

Are used to form the future tense of verbs; as, He *will* come. I *shall* leave you.

Shall should be used in the *first person*, and **will** in the *second* and *third* to denote *future* time; as, I *shall* go. You *will* go. He *will* go.

Will should usually be used in the *first person*, and **shall** in the *second* and *third*, to denote determination; as, I *will* go. You *shall* go. He *shall* go.

The same rules govern the use of *should* and *would* that govern the use of *shall* and *will*.

The principal difference between *shall* and *will*, in the second or third person, may be stated as follows: *Shall* implies duty and obligation that is prompted by the force of circumstances without the consent of the actor. *Will* implies willingness, purpose, intention, or determination of its subject. It is more courteous to say, "you will go," than "you shall go," because the former expression assumes your willingness, and the act proceeds from it; while the latter denotes compulsion. If I say, "you shall come," I assert that the coming is to take place without reference to willingness on your part.

Correct such of the following sentences as need correction:

1. Where will I leave him?
2. I will be drowned and nobody shall help me.
3. They requested that the appointment should be given to the man who knows his party.
4. I will never see him again.
5. When will we get through being punished?
6. Will I help you tomorrow?
7. I will be obliged to obey you.
8. I despise him but I will obey him.
9. He shall work today.
10. Will I bring you a glass of water?

NOTES.

1. Care should be taken to use such *forms of the verb* as will agree with the *person and number* of *its subject.*

2. The pronouns *we* and *you*, even when representing an individual, require the *same form* of the verb as the *plural noun.*

3. A verb having *two* or *more subjects* of different persons, agrees with the subject nearest to it ; as, He or *I am* going.

4. Do not use the *perfect participle* to express past time ; as, *I have done the work*, for, *I did the work.*

5. *Auxiliaries* are often improperly used before the past tense of verbs; as, I *have wrote* a letter, for, I *have written* a letter. He *has went* home, for, He *has gone* home.

6. If a verb has *two* or *more subjects* of different numbers connected by *or* or *nor* the subject in the plural is placed *nearest the verb*, and the verb *agrees* with *it;* as, He or his *friends are* going.

7. A verb having *two* or *more subjects*, mentioned or understood, must be of the form which *agrees* with a *plural noun;* as, *Truth, honor*, and *mercy, are* noble qualities.

8. If *two* or *more subjects* in the singular connected by *and* are used to denote but *one person or thing*, the verb should be of the form which *agrees* with a *singular noun;* as, That *statesmen* and *patriot merits* our gratitude.

9. If singular subjects connected by *and*, are preceded by *each, every, no*, or a *similar adjective*, they are considered separately, and require the same form of the verb as a singular noun; as, *Every nerve and sinew was strained* to make the offort.

10. *General truths* should be expressed in the *present tense;* as, He learned that the earth *is* round; not the earth *was* round.

11. If two or more subjects are connected by *as well as, and also, but not, etc.*, they belong to different propositions, and the verb mentioned agrees with the first, each of the others being the *subject* of a *verb understood;* as, The *mother, as well as* the child, *was saved.*

12. A verb having *two* or *more subjects* in the singular, connected by *or* or *nor* should be of that form which agrees with singular nouns; as *John or James is going*.

Correct the following sentences :

1. One or both of the boys is in the garden. 2. Having wrote the letter, he mailed it. 3. The torrid and the frigid zone represents the extremes of heat and cold. 4. Have the grammar class recited? 5. They, as well as I, am influenced by what he said. 6. Neither she nor you studies. 7. The ant and the bee is often cited as good examples of industry. 8. A number of persons were there. 9. The molasses are very nice. 10. You or Mary are mistaken. 11. The bear, as well as the deer, are nearly extinct in the eastern part of the United States. 12. Circumstances alters cases. 13. The assembly was divided in its opinion. 14. The committee were to examine the account. 15. He has not saw him. 16. The legislature have adjourned. 17. Each village and each hamlet have their petty chief. 18. She has tore her new bonnet. 19. I learned many years ago that the sun was a planet. 20. Neither her nor May are here.

VERB PHRASES.

A **True Verb** consists of one word, but frequently several words are taken together and used to perform the office of a verb. When such is the case, the entire expression is regarded as a *verb phrase*.

Verb Phrases are made up of one principal verb and one or more auxiliary verbs; as, *He may be punished*. The verb phrase " may be punished " is made up of the smaller verb phrase " may be " and the perfect participle of the verb " punish."

Forms of Verb Phrases.*

1. Do, does, or did ——
2. May, can, must, will, shall, might, could, should, or would ⎫ strike.
3. Am, is, are, was, or were — to strike.
4. Be, am, is, are, was, were
5. May, can, must, shall, will, might, could, should, or would be
6. Have, has, or had been —
7. May, can, must, shall, will, might, could, should, or would have been ⎫ striking.
8. Have, has, or had —
9. May, can, must, shall, will, might, could, should, or would have
10. Am, is, are, was, or were to have ⎫ struck.

A Passive Verb Phrase

Is one which represents its *subject acted upon* or *enduring an act*; as, *James* was struck by William.

The *passive verb phrases* are formed by placing some form of the verb " be " before the *perfect participle* of a verb which takes an object. *Passive verb phrases* do not take objects.

— - -

* These forms are *not* given for the *pupil to commit to memory* but merely as a matter of reference to assist in forming correct habits of speech. The teacher may mention some verbs and have the pupils use them with the proper auxiliaries, or have the pupils write essays containing all common verb phrases.

Forms of Passive Verb Phrases.

1. Be, am, is, are, was, or were
2. May, can, must, shall, will, might, could, should, or would *be*
3. Am, is, was, or were *to be*
4. Have, has, or had *been*
5. May, can, must, shall, will, might, could, should, or would *have been*
6. Was or were *to have been*

} *struck.*

The *object* of the verb becomes the *subject*, when the verb is changed into a *passive verb phrase*.

For example: John struck *Henry*. *Henry* was struck by John.

Write sentences containing the proper forms of the following verbs used both in an active and a passive sense: * *Teach*, *love*, *learn*, *study*, *cook*, *build*, *burn*, *pursue*, *kill*, and *write*.

The *tense* of a verb phrase is determined by the *auxiliary* verb.

Verb Phrases frequently end with words which are usually used as adverbs or prepositions; as, The farm *has been taken possession of* by the sheriff. He *was laughed at*. In the first sentence " has been taken possession of " is a verb phrase used as the predicate; in the second sentence " was laughed at " is a verb phrase used as the predicate.

How to Form Certain Verb Phrases.

In such sentences as the following: The house *is building;* The dinner *is cooking;* " is building " and " is

---

* In writing these sentences the pupils should use every possible auxiliary before them.

cooking" are passive verb phrases which represent their subject as being acted upon. Such expressions as the above are frequently doubtful in their meaning, and on this account another form of the verb phrase is usually preferred. The house *is being built*. The dinner *is being cooked*. The last form should always be used whenever the other would be doubtful in its meaning. We may say the dinner *is cooking* without danger of being misunderstood, but it is a great deal better to say The thief *is being punished*, than The thief *is punishing*.

EXERCISES.

1. Write two sentences illustrating the correct use of will in the first person; in the second; in the third. 2. Write sentences illustrating the correct use of may, can, must, might, could, would, and should. 3. Write four sentences containing passive verb phrases. 4. Write five sentences containing appositives. 5. Write four sentences containing phrases which modify the subject. 6. Write four sentences containing phrases which modify the predicate. 7. Write three sentences containing participial phrases. 8. Write four sentences containing infinitive phrases, and change the infinitive phrases into subordinate clauses.

Same Case After the Verb.

Incomplete Verbs requiring *attributes* should have the *same case* after them as before them when the word that follows them means the same as the subject.

NOTES.

1. The verbs which most frequently separate nouns and pronouns meaning the same person or thing are:

be, become, appear, grow, call, choose, consider, make,
etc. In such sentences as the following: I supposed *it* to
be *him*, the word " it " is in the objective case ; the subject of the infinitive " to be." Consequently the word
that follows the infinitive " him " is in the objective case;
but in the sentence, I thought *it* was *he*, the word " it "
is in the subjective case, the subject of the verb " was."
Consequently the noun or pronoun that follows the verb
is also in the subjective case.

2. A *noun* or *pronoun* used as the *attribute* of an *infinitive*, when the *subject* of the infinitive *is expressed*, is
commonly in the *objective case*. If, however, the subject
of the infinitive is not expressed or it is *the same* as the
subject of the *verb* and the infinitive is followed by a
noun or pronoun used *attributively*, the word following
is usually in the *subjective* or the *independent case;* as,
It was taken to be *he*.

It certainly could not have been thought to be *they*.

I wish to be *he*.

3. When the *participles* of any of the above verbs are
limited by a *possessive* and immediately followed by a
noun or *pronoun*, the *noun* or *pronoun* is in the *independent case;* as, The fact of *its* being *he* need not alter your
opinion.

4. In a clause expressing *doubt, supposition, desire* or
denial, if the verb is some form of the verb " be," it
should be of that form which agrees with a *plural noun.*
It matters not whether the subject is *singular* or *plural:*
as, *If I were you*, not, If I was you. *If I were he*, not
If I was he.

Correct the following sentences :

1. It could not have been her. 2. It was thought to
be him. 3. It was him that issued the order, although

6

the people for a long time disbelieved it to be he. 4. They believed it to be I. 5. I thought it was him. 6. That is her. 7. The court had no doubt of its being them who were guilty. 8. If I were him or her, I would improve the opportunities presented to me. 9. That's him. 10. If I had known it to be she, I would have spoken to her in a very different manner. 11. If I were her I would leave you. 12. I do not believe that I would consent if I was you. 13. Its being him is just what's the matter. 14. It is said to be him. 15. I supposed it to be she.

SIT, SET, LIE, AND LAY.

The complete verbs *sit* and *lie* convey the idea of rest or repose and should never have objects. The incomplete verbs *set* and *lay* express action and take objects. It is correct to say, He *set* the pitcher of water on the table, but it is not correct to say, He *set* down. The verb set is, however, properly used as an incomplete verb when we say, The stars *set*, or, the sun *sets*, but Mr. White has shown that set used in this way is a corruption of the verb *settle*.

Correct the following sentences:

1. The old man sets in his easy chair. 2. Here is setting room. 3. Take a chair and set down. 4. The ship lays at the wharf. 5. We sat forty peach trees in the orchard. 5. Please sit the pitcher on the shelf. 7. I have lain the book on the table. 8. He has laid down. 9. Tell him to go and lay down. 10. Myrtle has lain the book on the organ.

EXPECT, TEACH, AND LEARN.

Expect means to look for something which is to happen in the future. Do not use it in the sense of *conclude*, *suspect, suppose,* or *think.* It is correct to say I *expect* a friend to call on me to-morrow, but incorrect to say, I *expect* the earth is round.

Teach means to impart knowledge. *Learn* is to acquire it. Care should be taken not to misuse them.

Correct the following:

1. Please learn me how to knit.
2. I learned him grammar.
3. I expect you are angry with me.
4. I expect he is trying to injure me.
5. I expect I know my lesson.

EXERCISES.

Copy the following sentences, filling the blanks with some form of lie or lay:

The rain has —— the dust. He —— down to sleep. They have —— for three hours. Lydia —— book on my desk. I wish you would please —— letter down.

Copy the following sentences, filling the blanks with some form of sit or set:

Mr. Smith is —— out tomato plants. Will you —— by me? Please —— pitcher on the table. Who —— the table? She —— in the front row. I saw a man who was —— by the roadside. I wish you would —— pitcher down, and let it —— there. The physician has —— the boy's arm. The hen is —— on fifteen eggs.

EXERCISES FOR ANALYSIS.

I never thought of his doing the work.

This is a *simple sentence.*

" I " is a *pronoun* in the *singular number, first person,* and *subjective case;* the subject of " thought."

" Thought " is a *verb* in the *past tense,* used as the predicate of " I." " Of " is a *preposition* showing the relation between " thought " and " his doing the work." " His doing the work " is a *phrase* used as the *object* of the preposition " of."

" His " is a *pronoun,* in the *singular number, third person, masculine gender, possessive case,* and modifies " doing."

* " Doing " is a *participle used as a noun,* having " work " for its object. " The " is an *adjective* modifying " work." " Work " is a *common noun, singular number, third person,* and *objective case;* the object of " doing."

Doing may be called a *participle used as a noun* or a *participial noun.* Many grammarians insist that a distinction should be made in the use of these terms, but those who will take the trouble to investigate our standard authors on grammar will find that if there is such a distinction it cannot be conformed to the sentences given as examples by our grammarians. The following sentence is given in Goold Brown's Grammar of Grammars, page 239, to illustrate the *participial noun:* The *triumphing* of the wicked is short. The following one is given by Raub, page 204, to illustrate the *participle used as a noun:* Our *buying* the books so soon was commended. Both of these sentences are in direct violation of the laws laid down by those who attempt to refute the synonyms of these terms.

---

* In the above sentence " doing " may be disposed of as the *object* of the preposition " of " and " work " may be disposed of as the object of " doing." A *participial noun* may be used as the *object of a verb or preposition* and at the same time *govern an object.*

1. I do not remember its being she.
2. It is you to whom I am indebted for the favor.
3. I did not think of his striking me.
4. Money is scarce and times are hard.
5. He gave me a book.
6. I went home.
7. He taught me how to read.
8. He remained many years after returning home.
9. The orations of Cæsar were admired for strength and eloquence.
10. I saw the man, he of whom you spoke.
11. Few shall part where many meet.
12. The rain ceasing, a rainbow appeared.
13. The ship sinking, the crew were lost.
14. The dread of death arises from an illusion of the imagination.
15. In examining evidence, the mind should be unbiased.
16. No evil is so slight that it should not be avoided.
17. Whatever crushes individuality is despotism.
18. Those fighting custom with grammar are foolish.
19. The swan achieved what the goose conceived.
20. Authors must not, like Chinese soldiers, expect to win victories by turning summersets in the air.
21. Prayer is the key of the morning, and the bolt of night.
22. Worth makes the man ; want of it the fellow.
23. Puff balls have grown six inches in a single night.
24. They offered Cæsar the crown three times.
25. A dainty plant is the ivy green.
26. Alexander, the conqueror of the Persian empire, died at Babylon.
27. He who receives a good turn should never forget it ; and he who does one should never remember it.

28. Make proper use of your time; for the loss of it can never be regained.

29. He is a free man whom the truth makes free.

30. The eye is the window of the soul.

ADJECTIVES.

Comparison is a *statement* of the *different forms* of an *adjective*.

There are three degrees of comparison :

The *Positive* which expresses the simple quality.

The *Comparative* and the *Superlative* which are used in comparing objects which differ in degree.

The *Superlative* is said to express the highest or lowest degree of comparison, while the comparative seems to be a degree between the *positive* and *superlative*.

HOW COMPARED.

Words of one syllable are compared by suffixing *r* or *er* to the *positive*, to form the *comparative*, and *st* or *est* to the positive to form the *superlative;* as,

short,	shorter,	shortest.
fit,	fitter,	fittest.
wise,	wiser,	wisest.
hard,	harder,	hardest.
soft,	softer,	softest.

Many words of *two syllables* are compared the same as the words of one syllable ; as,

sincere,	sincerer,	sincerest.
able,	abler,	ablest.
handsome,	handsomer,	handsomest.

common,	commoner,	commonest.
pleasant,	pleasanter,	pleasantest.
guilty,	guiltier,	guiltiest.
holy,	holier,	holiest.
gentle,	gentler,	gentlest.
narrow,	narrower,	narrowest.
yellow,	yellower,	yellowest.

Words of *more* than one syllable are usually compared by placing *more* or *less* to the positive to form the *comparative;* and *most* or *least*, to the positive to form the *superlative* ; thus,

beautiful	more beautiful,	most beautiful
beautiful,	less beautiful,	least beautiful.
famous,	more famous,	most famous.
famous,	less famous,	least famous.
distant,	more distant,	most distant.
distant,	less distant,	least distant.

Some adjectives are compared irregularly; as,

good,	better,	best.
bad,	worse,	worst.
little,	less,	least.
fore,	former,	first.
late,	later,	last.
much,	more,	most.

There are |many adjectives, which according to their strictest sense, do not admit comparison; but they are often used with a certain latitude of meaning which renders their comparison admissible, and in accordance with the usages laid down by our best writers for centuries past.

We mention the following as examples :

* *Honest, true, correct, sincere, perfect, round, square, perpendicular,* and *inferior.*

NOTES.

Adjectives Relate to Nouns and Pronouns.

† 1. It is usually said that the comparative degree should be used when a comparison is made with two objects and the superlative degree when comparison is made with more than two objects; as, He is the better boy of the two.

He is the best boy of the three.

2. *A,* and *an,* can relate to nouns in the singular only, except when the words " few," " many," " dozen," "thousand," etc., come between them and the noun. Then they may relate to plural nouns; as, A *few* men, a *dozen* flies, etc.

---

* Knowing that it is hypercritically affirmed by many grammarians that these adjectives do not admit comparison, we beg to call the pupil's attention to the following sentences :

" And to render nations *more perfect* in the knowledge of it."— *Campbell's Rhet.,* p. 171. " No poet has ever attained a *greater perfection* than Horace."—*Blair's Lect.,* p. 393. " More wise, more learn'd, *more just,* more everything."—*Pope.* " From the first rough sketches, to the *more perfect* draughts."—*Bolingbroke on Hist.,* p. 152. " The *most perfect.*"— *Adam's Lect. on Rhet.,* i, 99 and 136; ii, 17 and 57 : *Blair's Lect.,* pp. 20 and 399.

† The above note is not strictly true as our best writers seem to take no particular cognizance of it even in their choicest productions.

3. *The* may relate to nouns in either the singular or plural number. *The* points things out definitely; *a* and *an* indefinitely. *A* should be used before consonant sounds; *an* before vowel sounds. *A* should be used before long *u;* as, He wore *a* uniform.

4. *A*, *an*, and *the* should be used before each of two or more adjectives in a series when they modify different nouns. When they modify the same noun they should be used but once; as, *An* intelligent and *a* white man, means *two* men. *An* intelligent and white man, means *one* man.

5. If a comparison is expressed between two nouns referring to the same person or thing, adjectives should be used before the first one only; as, He is *a better* editor than lawyer. The expression, He is *a* better editor than *a* lawyer, means that he is *a better editor* than a lawyer *is an editor.*

6. The adjective should not be used before the name of a species included in a class; as, The dog is a faithful kind of *an* animal, should be, The dog is a faithful kind of animal.

Notice the following expressions from standard authors:

" When our sentence consists of two members, the *longest* should, generally, be the concluding one." — *Blair's Rhet.*, p. 117: and *Jamieson's*, p. 99. " The *shortest* member being placed first, we carry it more readily in our memory as we proceed to the second." — *Ib.*, & *Ib.*

" In the *first* of these two sentences." — *Churchill's Gram.*, p. 162 ; *Lowth*, p. 120.

According to the rule given by many grammarians " first " in the above sentence should have been " former; " but this would be ambiguous because *former* might mean *maker*.

7. When the comparative degree is used, the latter term should never include the former ; as, He is *more* admired than any poet, should be, He is *more* admired than any *other* poet.

8. When the superlative degree is used, the latter term should always include the former; as, Longfellow is the *most* admired of all the *other* American poets, should be, Longfellow is the *most* admired of all the American poets.

9. Care should be taken in the arrangement of adjectives. There is quite a difference in the meaning expressed by the sentences, A lady's *black* glove, and A *black* lady's glove.

10. Avoid *double* comparatives and superlatives ; as, A *more sweeter* thought, should be, A *sweeter* thought.

The double comparative " lesser " is sanctioned by good authority; as, The *lesser* Asia.

11. Avoid using *adverbs* as adjectives ; as, The children feel *finely*, should be, The children feel *fine*. The stars look *brilliantly* to-night, should be, The stars look *brilliant* to-night.

12. It is bad English to say, Charles is *taller than any one* in the family, for he is one of the family, and this sentence makes him taller than himself. It should be, Charles is *taller than any one else* in the family. It is also bad English to say, George is the *tallest of his brothers;* for, he is not one of his own brothers, but this sentence makes him so. It should be, George is taller *than any of his brothers.*

13. There is authority for using interchangeably the expression, the *first two*, the *two first;* the *last three*, and the *three last.*

Correct the following sentences:

1. Mary is the tallest of her sisters.

2. Noah and his family outlived all the people who lived before the flood.

3. The flea is stronger than any insect of its kind.

4. The dove is a peaceabler bird than the jay.

5. Reason was given to a man to control his passions.

6. No person was ever so perplexed as he has been to-day.

7. John behaves very civil.

8. I would go a long ways to hear him speak.

9. He gave me a large and small knife.

10. Franklin was no less a statesman than a philosopher.

11. That was a awful accident.

12. The black and the white horse was injured by his fall.

13. My father thought me worse than any of his children.

14. I have the most elegantest hat.

15. Words taken independent of their meaning are parsed as nouns in the neuter gender.

16. The title of a duke was bestowed upon Wellington.   .

17. The tall and short man were in the street together.

18. The sweet and sour apple came from the same orchard.

19. He writes remarkably elegant.

20. Rhode Island is smaller than any State of the Union.

21. He is a wise and a true man.

22. Webster was a more celebrated orator than a statesman.

EACH, EVERY, EITHER, AND NEITHER.

The above adjectives require the nouns which they modify to be in the singular.

1. EACH is used to denote two or more objects taken separately; as, *Each* man is entitled to his share. Grass grows on *each* side of the road.

2. EVERY is applied to more than two objects taken separately, but comprehends them all, as, *Every* man is known by his actions. *Every* is sometimes joined to a plural noun; as, *Every* ten years.

3. EITHER and NEITHER are used to refer to *two objects* only; as, Either of the *two* apples. Instead of saying, *Either* of the *fifty* men, say, *Any* of the fifty men.

Correct the following sentences:

1. Trees grow on every side of the creek. 2. Take either of the twenty apples. 3. Neither of the three girls were there. 4. Each tree is known by its fruit. 5. There is nice grass on every bank of the river.

THIS, THAT, THESE, THOSE, ETC.

1. *This* and *that* refer to singular nouns. *These* and *those* to plural nouns. *This*, and its plural *these*, are used in speaking of things near us, or things last referred to. *That* and its plural *those*, are used in speaking of things at a distance, or things first referred to.

2. The pronoun *them* is often improperly used for the adjective *those;* as, Them peaches are good, should be, Those peaches are good.

3. When the noun is plural the adjective which modifies it must be plural; as *six miles, thirty dollars.*

4. Some nouns used collectively retain the singular form, though limited by a plural noun. Thus, *Forty head* of cattle. A fleet of *forty sail.*

5. When a compound adjective consists of an adjective and a noun, the noun part retains the singular form ; as, A *ten-cent* piece. A *three-month* scholarship.

6. Do not use *this here* and *that there* for *this* and *that*.

Correct the following sentences:

1. Those are good molasses.
2. Them apples are nice.
3. Will you drive them cattle out of the yard?
4. Those kind of apples is sweet.
5. Neither of them three men were in the room.
6. Did you place them books on the shelf?
7. The boy ran six mile an hour.
8. The lot is bounded on the south by a sixteen-feet alley.
9. A herd of ninety heads of cattle are grazing on the meadow.
10. Sallie took a twelve-months scholarship.
11. Give me that there book.
12. He bought a four-years old horse.

ADVERBS.

Be careful to place adverbs where they will express the meaning intended.

NOTES.

1. When the adverbs, WHENCE, THENCE, WHERE, THERE, etc., are preceded by the preposition *from* they become nouns. Thus the expression, " From *whence* cometh my help?" means, " FROM WHAT PLACE cometh my help?" It would be more elegant to omit " from," for when the adverb *whence* is used, the idea conveyed by the preposition is implied.

2. The *adverb* should not be used as the *attribute* of a verb. It cannot modify the subject ; as, The city looks *gaily*, should be, The city looks *gay*.

3. Usually the adverbs *very* and *too*, should not modify participles; as, I was *too enraged* to speak, should be, I was *too much enraged* to speak.

4. Do not use two negative words to express a negation ; as, I *haven't nothing* to do, should be, I *haven't anything* to do, or I *have nothing* to do.

5. Do not use *that* instead of *so;* as, He is *that* proud that he will not speak to us, should be, He is *so* proud that he will not speak to us.

6. * Never put any word between *to* and its verb ; such expressions as, *To not know*, should be *Not to know*.

---

* Of the infinitive verb and its preposition *to*, some grammarians say, that they must never be separated by an adverb. It is true, that the adverb is, in general, more elegantly placed before the preposition than after it ; but, possibly, the latter position of it may sometimes contribute to perspicuity, which is more essential than elegance ; as, " If any man refuse *so to implore*, and *to so receive* pardon, let him die the death." *Fuller on the Gospel*, p. 209. The latter word *so* if placed like the former, might possibly be understood in a different sense from what it now bears. But perhaps it would be better to say, " If any man refuse so to implore, and *on such terms* to receive pardon, let him die the death." " Honor teaches us *properly* to respect ourselves." — *Murray's Key*, ii, 252. Here it is not quite clear, to which verb the adverb "*properly*" relates. Some change of the expression is therefore needful. The right to place an adverb sometimes between *to* and its verb, should, I think, be conceded to the poets : as, " Who dare *to nobly stem* tyrannic pride." — *Burns: C. Sat. N.*

From *Goold Brown's Grammar of Eng. Gram.*, p. 661.

7. *As — as*, is used to *express equality;* as, He is *as* good *as* I. *So — as*, is used to *deny equality;* as, He is *not so* good *as* I.

8. Do not use *where* for *when;* as, *Where* a man tries to do right, he should be encouraged, should be, *When* a man tries to do right, he should be encouraged.

9. Avoid using *no* for *not;* as, Did he come or *no*, should be, Did he come or *not*.

10. When the adverb " ever " follows such words as " seldom " and " rarely " it is preceded by " if " and the adverb never in such cases, is preceded by " or ;" thus: *Seldom if ever. Rarely or never.*

11. In the use of *only* and *not only* we should be careful to place them so as to express the meaning intended, as, *Only* they marched an hour. In this sentence *only* is an adjective modifying *they*. They *only* marched an hour. In this sentence *only* is an adverb modifying *marched*. They marched an hour *only*. Here *only* is an adjective modifying *hour*.

12. Many adverbs are compared the same as adjectives. Thus, *often, oftener, oftenest; fast, faster, fastest; soon, sooner, soonest; frequently, more frequently, most frequently.*

13. The adverbs *yes, no, etc.*, when used in answer to questions, are usually equivalent to entire propositions. They may, however, be disposed of as adverbs used independently.

EXERCISES.

Correct the following:

1. That dress looks prettily upon her.
2. My head feels badly.
3. She looks neatly.
4. He learns easy.
5. Feathers feel softly.

6. He doesn't know nothing.
7. He intended to often visit me.
8. I was that faint that I could hardly walk.
9. They were nearly dressed alike.
10. You walk too slow.
11. Nobody suspects you ever.
12. The tortured man begged that they would kill him again and again.
13. The children feel finely.
14. I only have one apple.   .
15. I never saw a dog with such a bushy tail before.
16. Pupils should be taught to carefully spell the words.   .
17. I have thought of marrying often.
18. Charlie can't nowhere be found.
19. She can look gracefully in that dress.
20. I cannot see to write no more.

CONJUNCTIONS

Connect the sentences, parts of sentences, and words between which they are placed.

Co-ordinate Conjunctions connect sentences or * elements of *equal* rank; as, James went, *but* John stayed at home; He is a studious *and* intelligent boy.

† **Subordinate Conjunctions** connect elements of *unequal* rank ; as, He will teach us *if* he has time; He left *because* his life was in danger.

---

* An element is a part of a sentence. It may be a word, a phrase, or a clause.

† We will here state that no sharp line of distinction can be drawn between subordinate conjunctions and conjunctive adverbs. A similar note is also given by Mr. Whitney in Whitney's Essentials of Eng. Gram., p. 150.

Co-ordinate Conjunctions.

also,	nay,
although,	neither,
and,	neither — nor,
besides,	nor,
both,	nor — nor,
*both — and	now,
but,	or,
either,	or — or,
either — or	otherwise,
else,	so,
further,	still,
furthermore,	through,
likewise,	yet,
moreover,	

Subordinate Conjunctions.

After,	however,	than,
as,	if,	that,
as — as,	if — then,	then,
as — so,	inasmuch as,	therefore,
as well as,	in case,	though — yet,
because,	notwithstanding,	thus,
but,	provided,	unless,
except,	since,	wherefore,
for,	so — as,	
howbeit,	so — that,	

* Such conjunctions as *both — and*, *either — or*, *neither — nor*, *as — as*, *so — as*, etc., are called corresponsives.

7

NOTES.

1. There is generally an ellipses in a clause connected by *as* or *than*. The noun or pronoun following these words is usually the *subject* of a *suppressed verb;* as, He is farther advanced than *I*, means that, He is farther advanced than *I am advanced*.

2. When *words* or *clauses* are connected by *corresponsives*, care should be taken to make the *right* selection.

3. Words having the form of conjunctions, and used to introduce sentences are called *expletives*.

4. Do not use *where* instead of *which* in reference to what is not strictly place. It is correct to say, This is the place *where* I saw him, but the sentence, I know the page *where* the mistake may be found, should be, I know the page *on which* the mistake may be found.

5. Do not use *and* instead of *to* before the infinitive; as, Try *and* behave yourself, should be, Try *to* behave yourself.

Correct the following sentences:

1. Try and come to-morrow. 2. This is the letter where he speaks of his journey. 3. Neither the man or his horse was found. 4. It was no other but his father. 5. He would neither do it himself or let me do it. 6. Where a man tries to do what is right he ought to be encouraged. 7. Did you say this is so good as that? 8. Try and do your duty cheerfully. 9. The book is not as well printed as it ought to be. 10. I could not but buy it, only borrow it. 11. This is not as new as that. 12. Cornwallis could not do otherwise but surrender.

PREPOSITIONS

Show the relation between their *object* and some *other word*.

List of Prepositions.

a,	between,	past,
abaft,	betwixt,	pending,
aboard,	beyond,	per,
about,	but,	respecting,
above,	by,	round,
across,	concerning,	save,
adown,	despite,	saving,
after,	during,	since,
against,	ere,	till,
along,	except,	to,
amid,	excepting,	touching,
amidst,	far,	toward,
among,	from,	towards,
amongst,	in,	under,
around,	into,	underneath,
as,	like,	unlike,
aslant,	near,	until,
astride,	next,	unto,
at,	nigh,	up,
athwart,	notwithstanding,	upon,
before,	of,	versus,
behind,	off,	via,
below,	on,	with,
beneath,	opposite,	within,
beside,	over,	without,
besides,		

aboard of,	as to,
as for,	but for,

from among,   in place of,
from between,   in respect to,
from off,   on account of,
from under,   previous to,
out of,   in spite of,
over against,   with respect to,
according to,   in the relation of,
contrary to,   in the character of,
devoid of,   to the extent of, etc.,
in consideration of,   regardless of,
instead of,

Remark. The pupil will please bear in mind that many words in the above list are also used as other parts of speech.

Care should be taken to use *such prepositions* as express the *relations intended.*

A few of the most important combinations of prepositions are here given:

Abstain *from.*

Access *to.*

Accompanied *by, with.*

Account *of, for, to.*

Accuse *of.*

Admit *of.*

Agree *with* a person ; *to* things proposed ; *upon* things or conditions.

Allude *to.*

Angry *with* a person ; *at* a thing.

Apply *to.*

Approve *of.*

Believe *in, on.*

Bestow *on, upon.*

Call *on* a person ; *at* a place ; *for* a thing.

Concur *with* a person ; *in* opinion.

Confide *in.*

Copy *from* a thing ; *after* a person.

Correspond *to, with.*

Dictate *to.*

Die *of* a disease ; *by* the sword ; *for* another.

Differ *with* or *from* a person in opinion; *from* a person or thing in some quality.

Different *from*.

Disagree *to* a proposal; *with* a person.

Equivalent *to*.

Equal *to*, *with*.

Expelled *from*.

Independent *of*.

Intimate *with*.

Inseparable *from*.

Listen *for* expected sound; *to* present sound.

Negotiate *with*.

Preferable *to*.

Profit *by*.

Proud *of*.

Reconcile a thing *with*; a person *to*.

Rejoice *at* or *in* news; *with* a person.

Rid *of*.

Smile *on* favorably; *at* unfavorably.

Sneer *at*.

Sorry *for*.

Strive *with* a person; *for* an object.

Thankful *for*.

True *to*.

Void *of*.

Wait *on*, *upon*, *for*, *at*.

Useful *to* a person; *for* a purpose.

NOTES.

1. *Between* refers to two objects or sets of objects, *among*, to more than two.

2. Such expressions as *in short*, *in fine*, etc., may be used as adverb phrases, or *short* and *fine* may be disposed of as nouns in the objective case, object of the preposition *in*.

3. Two prepositions sometimes come together; as, the stream flows *from between* the rocks. They are then called compound prepositions.

4. *Into*, should be used after a verb denoting entrance; as, I put my knife *into* my pocket.

5. We differ *with* or *from* a person in opinion, *from* him in looks.

From, is used after the verb *differ*, but never after *to* or *than*.

6. In such sentences as, He went *a fishing*, and He went *a hunting*, *a* is used as a preposition.

7. *But* when used in such a construction as " all *but* me " is often considered a conjunction.

But, however, in cases of this kind is an old preposition meaning *without* or *except*, and all modern authorities favor its use in a prepositional sense.

8. The Latin prepositions *per*, *versus*, and *via* are employed in some technical expressions; as, " Fourteen dollars *per* barrel; " " Smith *versus* Jones; " " Go *via* the M., K. & T."

9. The words *worth*, *like*, *unlike*, *near*, *next*, and *nigh*, are considered prepositions by some of our very best grammarians; the pupil may, however, supply a preposition and consider them as other parts of speech. Thus, He sat *near* (to) the wall; He is not *like* (unto) his brother.

10. Care should be taken to construct sentences so that they will express the meaning intended to be conveyed.

For example, *Run away — A hired man named John; his nose turned up five feet eight inches high.* This sentence should be reconstructed. It may be expressed thus; Run away — A hired man named John. His nose turns up, and he is five feet eight inches high.

Correct the following sentences:

1. I differ to you in that opinion.

2. For sale, a piano, by a gentleman with richly carved rosewood legs, who is about to sail for Europe.

3. The soldiers were perishing for thirst.

4. My circumstances are different to yours.

5. The twelve men began to quarrel between themselves.

6. The soil is adapted for cotton and tobacco.

7. You may safely confide on him.

8. I was at London when this happened.

9. Lettie came in the room unobserved, and set down on a chair.

10. Dan and Charlie have gone in the garden to take a walk.

11. The'teacher compared this book to them.

12. Wanted a young man to take care of some horses of a religious turn of mind.

13. He rode to town and drove twelve cows on horseback.

14. A public dinner was given to the inhabitants of roast-beef and plum-pudding.

INFINITIVES.

The infinitive is a form of the verb which may be used as a *noun*, an *adjective*, or an *adverb*.

* The *subject* of an infinitive is usually in the objective case ; as, I took *James* to be John. He thought *him* to be a lawyer.

* When the subject of the infinitive is the *same* as the *subject* of the *verb limited by the infinitive*, the subject of the infinitive is in the subjective case. For example: John expected *to buy* a horse. It was supposed *to be* he. It is extremely doubtful whether this exception need be considered by the ordinary student of grammar, since so far as we have to do practically with the subject of the infinitive it is in the objective case. In instances of this kind and many others it seems to simplify matters to consider the infinitive as used without any particular subject.

1. *To* is the sign of the infinitive, and should never be separated from it. The sign *to*, however, is omitted after the verbs, *bid, dare, feel, hear, make, need, see, let, etc.,* and sometimes after *please, have,* and *help.*

2. The infinitive without *to* is also frequently used after *had rather, had better, had as lief, etc.;* as, He *had rather go.* You *had better* stay. I *had as lief* work as play. In the first sentence " he " is the subject, " had " is the predicate, modified by " rather," an adverb. " To go " is an infinitive, the sign " to " being omitted. The above expressions though frequently criticised, are sanctioned by good authority. All inconsistencies, however, may be avoided by using *would* instead of had.

3. Every *infinitive* and *participle* has the construction of a *noun, adjective,* or *adverb.*

4. A noun or pronoun preceding an infinitive should be considered the subject of the infinitive, when the *infinitive phrase* can be changed into a clause, and the *clause used as the subject* or *the object* of a verb.

For example, For a man to be proud of *his learning* is the greatest ignorance. John wishes *Mary to go.*

If we substitute a clause for the infinitive phrase in the first sentence, the sentence would read "That *a man should be proud of his learning* is the greatest ignorance," and the second sentence will read, " John wishes that *Mary should go,*" here it is evident that the words " man " and " Mary " are used as *subjects* of *infinitives.*

5. Some *infinitives* and *participles* when used as *nouns* are often followed by a *noun* or *pronoun* in the *independent* case; as, to be *he* is to be a *scholar.*

I never thought of its being *they.*

6. Usually the *present tense* of the infinitive should be

used with the *past tense* of the verb, and the *past tense* of the infinitive should be used with the *present tense* of the verb ; as, Milton *seems to have had* a wonderful imagination.

The miller was bound *to return* the flour.

7. When several infinitives come together, *to* is often used before the first and omitted before the others ; as, They come *to see, hear,* and *judge* for themselves.

8. The sign *to* of the infinitive should not be used alone for the full *infinitive form.* For example, I did not go nor do I intend *to,* should be, I did not go nor do I intend *to do so.*

Correct the following sentences:

1. We shall find the practice perfectly accord with the theory.

2. I saw him to write on his slate.

3. He made the horses to go very fast.

4. It is unjust to so decide the case.

5. It is better to suffer wrongfully than be guilty of wrong.

6. Come and visit me soon.

7. We were directed to go but we did not wish to.

8. We ought not to try and over-define or prove God.

9. He was heard say that the train was late.

10. It is wrong to not study our lessons.

11. To not attend is to not remember.

12. I never voted that ticket, and I never intend to.

13. He did no more than it was his duty to have done.

14. I found him better than I expected to have found him.

15. I wished to have gone with my friends into the country, but I was forbidden to.

PARTICIPLES.

The **Participle** IS A VARIATION OF THE VERB, sharing its nature, but used as an *adjective*, or a *noun*, or part of a *verb-phrase*.

The **Imperfect Participle** is one that expresses *unfinished action, or condition*, at the time indicated by the verb in the sentence ;

As, The evening train, *turning* a sharp curve was thrown from the track.

The **Perfect Participle** is one that expresses the *action or condition as completed or finished* at the time indicated by the verb ;

As, A tree *overturned* by the wind, lay across our path.

Notes on the Participle.

1. * The *Perfect Participle* should never be used instead of *past tense* to express past time ; as, Henry *seen* him do it, should be Henry *saw* him do it.

2. The adjective *the* should precede a *participial noun* and the preposition *of* should follow, or they *both* should be omitted; as, He delights in studying *of* grammar ; should be, He delights in *the* studying *of* grammar; or, He delights in studying grammar.

3. The meaning is usually the same when *the* is used before and *of* after a participial noun as when they are omitted ; but such is not always the case; for there is a

---

* The pupil should consult the dictionary whenever he is in doubt as to the perfect participle or past tense form of a verb. For the benefit of those, however, who have no dictionary convenient, we have, with much labor, arranged a list of irregular verbs and placed it in the appendix to this work.

great difference in the meaning expressed by, The man was ruined *by* burning his house, and, The man was ruined *by the* burning *of* his house.

4. When the *participle* is used as a *noun* it is frequently limited by a *possessive:* as, They tried to prevent *his* going.

The * *objective* is often used for the *possessive;* as, They tried to prevent *him* going.

5. *Do not use a Participial Noun* when the meaning can be more elegantly expressed by the use of an *infinitive* and its *object;* as, *Reading* poetry properly requires a knowledge of the author's meaning, would better be, *To read* poetry properly, requires a knowledge of the author's meaning.

---

* Our authors, good and bad, critics and no critics, with few exceptions, write sometimes the *objective* case before the participle, and sometimes the *possessive*, under precisely the same circumstances.— *Goold Brown's Gram. of Eng. Grammars*, p. 643.

We wish to say in reference to the above that a careful research has only served to convince us of the truthfulness of Mr. Brown's assertion, and while each form, no doubt, is sometimes used when the other would be preferable, still it is very hard to draw the line of distinction.

In the above sentences the meaning expressed is very nearly if not quite the same in either case, but there is considerable difference in the meaning expressed by, There is no harm in *children* playing by the river, and, There is no harm in *children's* playing by the river. The first sentence asserts that the *children* are not harmful, while the second asserts that the *act of their playing* is not harmful.

EXERCISES.

Correct the following sentences:

1. The teacher forbid them playing during the time set apart for the studying their lessons.

2. After writing his letters he commenced writing of his composition.

3. John says he seen his friends pass by.

4. I seen him yesterday.

5. We have saw much better times.

6. They had just went to home.

7. He sent a letter wrote on foolscap.

8. The audience expressed the pleasure which they experienced in the hearing the lecture.

9. Arnold done an act which will forever leave a blot upon his name.

10. The water in the pail is froze solid.

11. They refused doing so.

12. To attempt proving that thing is right.

*Exercises containing a general summary of the use of words, phrases, and clauses.

Participles: *Having done* the work, he went away. *Having been seen*, he departed.

Participles having adverbial modifiers: Words *once uttered*, cannot be recalled. He remained sitting *where we left him*. Reading, *without reflection*, does little good.

Participles having objects: Saving *time* is lengthening life. Expecting *to hear from you*, I did not leave.

----

* The teacher may require these sentences to be diagramed or analyzed.

The man denies *having* taken the *book*. *Having* said *what he thought*, he left.

Participles having complements : Being *weary*, I went home early. He, being a *loafer*, was not admitted. Having become *chairman*, he called the meeting to order.

Participles modified by Possessives : *Myra's* leaving was much regretted. By *his* stealing, he brought disgrace on his family. Pardon *my* bothering you.

Participles used as the subject of a verb: *Being criticised* is unpleasant. *Riding* is good exercise.

Participles used as the object of a verb: I enjoy *singing*. Avoid *reading trashy literature*. He remembers *having seen you*. The man regrets *having committed the deed*.

Participles used as complements of a verb : Seeing is *believing*. The trouble is *getting started*. Loving thy neighbor as thyself is *keeping the commandments of the Bible*.

Participles used as the objects of prepositions : Tired of *reading*, he went to sleep. The trouble lies in *tying the dog*. The arm grows from *being used*.

Participles used as adjective modifiers : Truth, *crushed to earth*, shall rise again. *Having learned his lesson*, he went to sleep.

Participles used with a noun or pronoun in an independent construction : *The sun being risen*, we pursued our journey. *The rain having ceased*, we went home. *The music having stopped*, we soon left.

Participles used as adjective attributes : The vine lies *withering* on the ground. The man returned *amazed*. Sallie went away *singing*.

Infinitives having adverbial modifiers : He tries to learn *rapidly*. We hope to see you *when you return*.

Infinitives having objects: He came to see *what he wanted.* Try to love your *enemies.*

Infinitives having complements: Mr. Whaley seems to be *very studious.* To be *happy* is a great blessing. Lorian desires to be *president.*

Infinitives used as the subject of verbs: *To err* is human; *to forgive,* divine. *To have a lovely disposition* is a great blessing.

Infinitives used as the object of verbs: We wish *to go.* Learn *to control your temper.*

Infinitives used as the complements of verbs: Clay's desire is *to be a good grammarian.* Mr. Johnson seems *to have been a smart man.*

Infinitives used as objects of participles: There is such a thing as trying *to do too much.* Learning *to wait,* is a difficult task.

Infinitives used adjectively: Flowers have their time *to bloom.* It is time for him *to stop.*

Infinitives used adverbially: We went *to see the city.* It is not easy *to do well.*

* **Infinitives used appositively:** It is not pleasant *to have so much rain.* It is almost impossible *to stop a malicious tongue.*

EXERCISES.

1. Write three sentences containing present participles.
2. Write three sentences containing perfect participles.
3. Write three sentences containing participles with adverbial modifiers. 4. Write two sentences containing participles used as complements. 5. Write two sentences using participles as objects of prepositions. 6. Write

---

* In these sentences, the infinitive is the real subject, and " it " is disposed of as being in apposition with the infinitive.

two sentences using participles as adjectives. 7. Write four sentences using infinitives in apposition with introductory " it." 8. Write two sentences containing infinitives with adverbial modifiers. 9. Write two sentences containing infinitives with objects. 10. Write two sentences containing infinitives used as objects of participles. 11. Write three sentences containing participles used in an independent construction. 12. Write four sentences containing participles limited by possessives. 13. Write three sentences containing infinitive phrases used as the subjects of verbs. 14. Write three sentences containing infinitives followed by adjective compliments. 15. Write three sentences containing participial phrases used as objects of verbs.

* *Substantive Phrases:* *To love the good* is a Christian trait. *Knowing what to say* secured him the position. He desires *to visit the World's Fair.*

Phrases used adjectively : A desire *to do good* is noble. A love *for the beautiful* is indicative of culture.

Phrases used adverbially: Flowers bloom *on the hill side.* She will come *next spring.* I shall be glad *to accompany you.*

† Substantive Clauses: Tell me *why you did it.* Gallileo taught *that the earth is round.* They asked *who he was.*

Clauses used adjectively : I have a friend *whom I wish you to meet.* She has a ring *of which she may justly be proud.* He dreamed of the hills *over which he roamed in the days of his youth.*

---

* A substantive phrase does the work of a noun.

† A substantive clause is a clause used to do the work of a noun.

Clauses used adverbially : He died *where he fell*. *If you wish to succeed*, persevere.

Clauses used as subjects : *When it was discovered* is unknown. *Whatever you want* you shall have. *How he did it* remains a mystery.

Independent constructions : *The cyclone having passed*, we continued our journey. *That being lost*, all is lost. *He having departed*, we soon fell asleep. *By the way*, I saw you yesterday. *To tell the truth*, I do not like her.

Parenthetical expressions having independent construction: The boat leaps, *as it were*, from billow to billow. He knows, *come what may*, I shall be true to him.

EXERCISES.

1. Write three sentences containing clauses used as subjects.

2. Write three sentences containing clauses used as attributes.

3. Write three sentences containing phrases used adjectively.

4. Write three sentences containing phrases used adverbially.

5. Write three sentences containing clauses used as objects.

6. Write two sentences containing participial phrases used independently.

7. Write two sentences containing parenthetical phrases used independently.

8. Write two sentences containing elements independent by pleonasm.

9. Write two sentences containing elements independent by address.

10. Write your own definition of a complex sentence.

11. Write your own definition of a compound sentence.

*General Exercises in Analysis.

1. They shall, every man turn to his own people, and flee every one into his own land.

In the first clause *man* is in apposition with *they.*

In the second clause *one* is in apposition with *they* understood.

If the pupils use diagrams, the teacher should insist upon full and lucid explanations, or the pupil may learn to diagram without having a clear idea of the exact relations of many of the words.

We are indebted principally to Holbrook, Harvey, Rhaub, and Reed & Kellogg for the great variety of sentences here produced.

2. The best part of our knowledge is that which teaches us where knowledge leaves off and ignorance begins.

That is an adjective, here used as a common noun, the attribute of the verb *is.*

Which is a conjunctive pronoun, the subject of *teaches,* and stands for *that.*

Us is the object of the preposition *to* understood.

The direct objects of *teaches* are : *knowledge leaves off where* and *ignorance begins where.*

Leaves off may be disposed of as a verb phrase, or *off* may be called an adverb.

---

* The pupil should be required to analyze or diagram all of the above sentences. We have simply given a few words of explanation to assist the student on difficult points and our remarks are in nowise intended as a full explanation of the sentences.

3. Three times seven are twenty-one.

This sentence may be disposed of by any one of the following methods:

(a) Three times *of* seven are twenty-one.

(b) Three times *of* seven *units* are twenty-one *units*.

(c) Seven *units taken to the number of* three times are twenty-one *units*.

. 4. All this I heard as one half dead: but answer had I none to words so true, save tears for my sins.

As may be disposed of as a preposition having *person* understood for its object, or a verb may be supplied and *as* will be a conjunctive adverb, thus: I heard *as* one half dead *hears.*

Save is a preposition having *tears* for its object.

All and *this* are adjectives modifying information understood.

5. I dare do all that may become a man; who dares do more is none.

The sign *to* of the infinitive is omitted after the **verb** *dare.*

He understood is the subject of the verb *is.*

Man and *none* are attributes.

6. Our very hopes belied our fears,
    Our fears our hopes belied;
    We thought her dying when she slept,
    And sleeping when she died.

Dying is a participle modifying *her*, and *sleeping* is a participle modifying *her* understood.

She slept when is a clause used to modify *thought.*

When is a conjunctive adverb.

7. There are moments, I think, when the spirit receives.
    Whole volumes of thought on its unwritten leaves.

There is an expletive or an introductory adverb.

When the spirit receives, etc., is a clause used to modify moments.

When is a conjunctive adverb and as here used is equivalent to *in which*.

The pupil will please remember that a few conjunctive adverbs seem to have the force of conjunctive pronouns, and when such is the case the conjunctive adverb connects back to a noun.

8.   Let beeves and home-bred kine partake
     The sweets of Burn-mill meadow;
     The swan[1] on still St. Mary's lake
     Float[1] double, swan[2] and shadow.

The sign *to* of the infinitive is omitted before *float*.

Swan [*to*] *float,* etc., is the object of *let* understood. *Swan*[2] and *shadow* are the objects of the preposition *as* understood, or they may be considered as in apposition with *swan*[1].

Double is an adjective used as the attribute of *float*.

9. Consider the lilies of the field, how they grow.

How they grow modifies *consider*. *How* is a conjunctive adverb. This sentence means *Consider the lilies of the field with respect to the manner in which they grow.*

10. Yet man is born into trouble, as the sparks fly upward.

Yet is an introductory conjunction.

As is a conjunctive adverb modifying *fly*.

11. It is he[1], even he[2].

Even may be considered an adverb modifying *is; he*[2] being in apposition with *he*[1], or *even* may be disposed of as a conjunction, the meaning being, *It is he even* [it is] *he.*

12. In Holland the stork is protected by law, because it eats the frogs and worms that would injure the dykes.

Because is a subordinate conjunction and the clause which it introduces modifies *is protected*. *That* is a conjunctive pronoun having *frogs* and *worms* for its antecedent.

13. There is a class among us so conservative that they are afraid the roof will come down if you sweep off the cobwebs.

There is an expletive.

Conservative modifies class, and *so* modifies conservative.

That is a subordinate conjunction and the clause which it introduces modifies *so*.

The clause *if you sweep, etc.*, modifies *will come*. *Off* is an adverb modifying *sweep*.

14. He that allows himself to be a worm must not complain if he is trodden on.

He is the subject of *must complain*. *Himself* is the subject of the infinitive *to be*. The clause *if he is trodden on* modifies *must complain*.

Is trodden on may be considered a verb phrase, or *on* may be disposed of as an adverb.

15. We are as¹ near to heaven by sea as² by land.

Near is the attribute of *are*. *As*¹ modifies near.

*As*² is a subordinate conjunction, and the clause which it introduces, [we are near] *by land*, modifies *as*.

16. Bear ye one another's burdens.

Ye is the subject, and *one* is in apposition with *ye*.

17. What made Cromwell a great man was his unshaken reliance on God.

"What" is the subject of "made." "Man" is a

noun in the objective case, used as the attribute of the infinitive " to be " understood. " What made Cromwell a great man " is a clause used as the subject of " was."

18. It is not always easy to make one's self just what one wishes to be.

To make one's self just what one wishes to be is the subject of *is,* and *it* is in apposition with the above clause. *Just* modifies *to make.*

What one wishes to be is a clause used as the factitive of *to make.*

What is a pronoun in the subjective case, used as the attribute of *to be.* *Self* is the object of *to make.*

19. An angel, if a creature of a day, What would he be.

Angel is in apposition with *he.*
If he were the creature of a day modifies *would be.*
If is a subordinate conjunction.

20. What matter how the night behaved?
    What matter how the north wind raved?

What may be disposed of as an adverb modifying *did matter,* *did* being understood, or it may be considered as an adjective modifying *matter.* *Matter* being used as the attribute of *was* understood. By the first method *matter* would be a verb, and by the second it would be a noun.

21. All were sealed with the seal which is never to be broken till the great day.

Till is a preposition. *Never* modifies *to be broken.*

22. Now blessing light on him that first invented sleep: it covers a man all over, thoughts and all, like a cloak.

Now is an introductory adverb.

Over is an adverb modifying *covers*, and *all* modifies *over*.

Thoughts and *all* (things) are in apposition with *man*. *Like* is a preposition.

23. I want to be quiet, and to be let alone.

Quiet and *alone* are adjectives used as attributes.

24. Then here's to our boyhood, its gold and its gray !
    The stars of its winter, the dews of its May !
    And when we have done with our life-lasting toys,
    Dear Father, take care of thy children, the boys !

The first part of this sentence means *Then here is* [a toast] *to our boyhood*.

Then is an introductory adverb.

Here is an adverb modifying *is*.

To is understood before, *its gold*, *its gray*, *stars*, and *dews*.

When we have done, etc., modifies *take*. *When* is a conjunctive adverb. *Care* is a noun.

Boys is in apposition with *children*.

25. I consent to the constitution, because I expect no better, and because I am not sure it is not best.

Sure is an adjective modified by the clause [that] *it is not best*. *That* is a subordinate conjunction understood. *Best* may be considered an adjective modifying a noun understood.

26. We meet in joy, though we part in sorrow ;
    We part to-night, but we meet to-morrow.

Though is a subordinate conjunction, and the clause which it introduces modifies *meet*. *But* is a co-ordinate conjunction. *To-night* and *to-morrow* are adverbs.

The first line forms a complex sentence; the second a compound sentence.

27. I never saw[1] a saw[2] saw[3] a saw[4] as that saw[5] saws[6] a saw[7].

Saw[1] is a verb ; *saw*[2] is a noun ; [to] *saw*[3] is an infinitive; *saw*[4] is a noun; *saw*[5] is a noun ; *saws*[6] is a verb; and *saw*[7] is a noun.

As is a conjunctive adverb, and the clause which it introduces modifies [to] *saw*[3].

As modifies *saws*[6].

28. The tutor said, in speaking of the word that[1], that[2] that[3] that[4] that[5] that[6] lady parsed, was not the that[7] that[8] that[9] gentleman requested her to analyze.

That[1] is a noun in apposition with *word*. *That*[2] is an expletive, and the clause which it introduces is the object of *said*. *That*[3] is an adjective modifying *that*[4]. *That*[4] is a noun, the subject of *was*. *That*[5] is a conjunctive pronoun the object of *parsed*. *That*[6] is an adjective modifying *lady*. *That*[7] is a noun, the attribute of *was*. *That*[8] is a conjunctive pronoun, the object of *to analyze*.

That[9] is an adjective modifying *gentleman*. The meaning would be plainer, if the sentence were written thus: The tutor said, in speaking of the word that, that that that which that lady parsed, was not the that which that gentleman requested her to analyze.

29. I feel my heart beating faster.

" Beating " is an adjective used as an attribute of "to be " understood, and modifies " heart." " Faster" is an adverb modifying " beating." " Heart " is the object of " felt."

30. The optic nerve passes from the brain to the back of the eyeball and then spreads out.

Then and *out* are adverbs modifying *spreads*.

31. For what is worth in anything
But so much money as 'twill bring?

For is an expletive.   *Worth* is a noun used as the subject.

In anything modifies *worth*.

But is a preposition, having *money* for its object.

As may be regarded as a conjunctive pronoun, having *money* for its antecedent.   It is used as the object of *will bring*.

32. I paid thirty-seven and a half cents for butter this morning.

Thirty-seven and a half is an adjective phrase, modifying *cents*.

33. Bird of the broad and sweeping wing,
    Thy home is high in heaven,
Where the wide storms their banners fling,
    And the tempest-clouds are driven.

Bird with its modifiers is used independently.

High is an adjective used as the attribute of *is*.

In heaven modifies *high*.

The last two lines modify *heaven*, *where* being a conjunctive adverb here used in the sense of a conjunctive pronoun.   *Where* modifies *fling* and *are driven*.

34. It was now the Sabbath day, and a small congregation of about a hundred souls, had met for divine service, in a place more magnificent than any temple that human hands had ever built to Deity.

Now modifies *was*.   *A hundred* may be called an adjective phrase modifying *souls*.

About modifies *a hundred*.

Than is a subordinate conjunction and the clause introduced by it modifies *more magnificent*.   *More* modifies *magnificent*.

Temple is the subject of a suppressed verb.

35. Many a morning on the moorlands did we hear the copses ring.

Many a modifies morning.

Morning is the object of a preposition understood. The sign *to* of the infinitive is understood before *ring*.

36. He that goes a[1] borrowing goes a[2] sorrowing.

A[1] and *a*[2] are prepositions, having the words following them for their objects.

37. Generally, also, a downright fact may be told in a plain way. *Generally* and *also* modify *may be told*.

38. Life is as[1] tedious as[2] a twice told tale.

Vexing the ears of a drowsy man.

Tedious is used as the attribute of the verb *is*. *As*[1] modifies *tedious*. *As*[2] is a conjunctive adverb, and the clause which it introduces modifies *tale*. *As*[2] modifies *is* understood. *Vexing* is a participle modifying *tale*.

39. Heaven is not gained at a single bound ;
But we build the ladder by which we rise
From the lowly earth to the vaulted skies,
And we mount to its summit round[1] by round.[2]

Rise is modified by the phrases *by which, from earth*, and *to skies*. *Mount* is modified by *to summit* and [with] *round*. ,

Round[1] is modified by the phrase *by round*.[2]

40. At midnight in his guarded tent,
The turk was dreaming of the hour,
When Greece, her knee in suppliance bent,
Should tremble at his power.

At midnight, in tent, and *of hour* modify *was dreaming*. The clause introduced by *when* modifies *hour*, *When* being a conjunctive adverb, and as here used is equivalent to *at which*. *Greece* is modified by the phrase

[with] *knee.   Knee* is modified by the participle *bent.
When* modifies *should tremble.*

Exercises for Analysis.

1. Let your communications be yea, yea, and nay,
nay.

2. Aptitude for business is not power of reason.

3. The streams of small pleasures fill the lake of
happiness.

4. A desire for knowledge is natural to the mind of
man.

5. He who masters his possessions conquers his
greatest enemies.

6. All that a man has will he give for his life.

7. John, kick the cat from under the table.

8. A teamster drove his horses too far into the river,
and in so doing he drowned them.

9. Soldier, rest ! thy warfare o'er,
   Dream of fighting fields no more. — *Scott.*

10. The way was long, the wind was cold,
    the minstrel was infirm and old. — *Scott.*

11. One ounce of gold is worth sixteen ounces of
silver.

12. They walk nearly across the bridge.

13. To reveal secrets or betray one's friends, is contemptible perfidy.

14. Sometimes her narrow kitchen walls
    Stretched away into stately halls. — *Whittier.*

15. Will you walk into my parlor, said the spider to
the fly?

16. Across the heath the owlet flew,
    And screamed along the blast.

17. Full many a promise rashly made
Is fated ne'er to be redeemed ;
Full many a duty long delayed,
Has lost to us a friend esteemed.

18. Thus many a sad to-morrow came and went.

19. He thought to learn to study to be to learn to think.

20. We one day descried some shapeless object floating at a distance.

21. A distinction ought to be made between fame and true honor.

22. Level spread the lake before him.

24. Refinement of mind and clearness of thinking usually result from grammatical studies.

24. And the night shall be filled with music,
And the cares that infest the day,
Shall fold their tents like the Arabs
And as quietly steal away.

25. Those who provide not for want, will find trouble.

26. How sweetly doth the moon beams smile,
To-night upon yon leafy isle.

27. The twilight hours like birds flit by.

28. The tongue is like a race-horse which runs the faster the less weight it carries.

MISCELLANEOUS EXERCISES.

Criticise the following sentences, making corrections when necessary :

1. I stopped but you were not at home.
2. I went a long ways yesterday.
3. Has the cattle been fed?
4. These kinds of cherries are good.
5. Them molasses are very fine.

6. I took it to be her.

7. They arrived safely.

8. John and I will go.

9. Him and I are old friends.

10. I thought it was them.

11. The horse, saddle and bridle were sold for one hundred dollars.

12. All who heard him, spoke well of him.

13. Three hundred and sixty-five days makes a year.

14. He is doing nice.

15. She looks beautifully.

16. That problem is very easy solved.

17. James and I went to the city.

18. Try and learn your lessons.

19. Some one has took my knife.

20. The thought is not as clearly expressed as it might be.

21. Our nation's safety rests upon the sobriety of its youth.

22. He is taller than her.

23. The rose smells sweet.

24. This is a remarkable pretty flower.

25. I have saw him twice.

26. He is the most funniest boy I have ever saw.

27. He or I is going to town.

28. We were setting on a log.

29. The sun is setting.

30. I will go to town to-morrow.

31. The boy has gone with the jailer.

32. I seed him as I came home.

33. Birds flees through the air.

34. Let the book lay on the table and come set down.

35. I know the page where the mistake may be found.

36. I don't know that I will go.

37. The pretty and ugly boy came to school.

38. I was very pleased to see you.

39. He is the most richest man I ever saw.

40. I never thought of it being her.

41. I knowed that it was him, for I seen him when he done it.

42. I feel that I cannot learn to write.

43. We sang a new hymn which we had never sang before.

44. Don't say nothing about it.

45. It is difficult to clearly understand him.

46. I did not say he is as good looking as his brother.

47. Books is a noun.

48. It was him.

49. A fine lot of umbrellas for sale by Brown & Jones having nicely carved ivory heads.

50. Capital, as well as men, were needed.

51. This here book is very interesting.

52. You and he stole the horse.

53. Here are the persons and things which we sent for.

54. Each of you shall have your part.

55. I didn't know the earth was round.

56. The water is ten foot deep.

57. They all come but him.

58. There comes the children.

59. I shall see whether I can go or not.

60. One of you are wrong.

61. Let each one try to do his best.

62. If you and me go the rest will follow.

63. If I were you I would not care.

64. Annie is the prettiest of her sisters.

65. It must be them.

66. It was me whom you saw.

67. Day's and Martin's blacking for sale here.

68. William reads rapidly.

69. She intends to break up housekeeping.

70. She spoke to James and I.

71. Take another example.

72. Do not let them know who I am.

73. Neither John nor James are remarkable for their talent.

74. No one knows better how to do it than him.

75. Who is at the door? Me.

76. The piece was much better recited by her than he.

77. The estate was to be equally divided between the six sons.

78. It certainly could not have been him.

79. This is the more better way to solve that problem.

80. Sallie and Mary are at home.

81. Neither the general nor his men were aware of their danger.

82. Having did the work faithfully he was rewarded.

83. I have saw him several time.

84. Who did you apply to?

85. The scissors is too large.

86. Us having returned they were happy.

87. These kind of oranges grow in Florida.

88. I, you, and John will go.

89. I made a very pleasant call this afternoon.

90. I seen her yesterday.

91. John is not so tall as him.

92. I will try to call on you this afternoon.

93. I shall be glad to see you at any time at which you may find it convenient to come.

94. Passengers are requested to not smoke in this car.

95. This is the Ladies entrance.

96. These sort of sentences need correcting.

97. He doesn't know nothing.

98. I would of gone, if he had of come.

99. They have came.

100. Those boys were farther down the road than us.

101. She sat by John and I.

102. A discussion arose between him and I as to who should have the prize.

103. A mule lost by a man with closely sheared mane and one lopped ear.

104. The best kind of a shade tree is the maple.

105. Each of you shall have your money.

106. We was there.

107. The ablest man who ever lived would not solve that problem.

108. Some deer was caught.

109. The number of students are increasing yearly.

110. Every chair, berth, and sofa were occupied.

111. Cæsar, as well as Cicero, were admired for their eloquence.

112. Every hour and every day have their appropriate duties.

113. I intended to have gone last week.

114. To be or not to be that is the question.

115. I seen the fire.

116. Has the train went by?

117. Beware of him who you know to be treacherous.

118. Wars occurred in Lincoln and Polk's administrations.

119. The pupil should be taught to carefully spell the words.

120. The farm was to be equally divided between the three boys.

121. As far as I am able to judge, the book is well written.

122. We told him to sit the cup by the bucket and set down.

123. This here book is not the one which I want.

124. We are doing fine in our new position.

125. Some one has stole my dog.

126. The witness seen the thief to enter the barn.

127. Neither despise the poor nor envy the rich.

128. They did not think of its being me.

129. Read the fourth and fifth page.

130. Every one must answer for themselves.

131. He is the wisest which lives the most nobly.

132. Every one should have her life insured.

133. I do not know whom they are.

134. I think I should have gone.

135. I knew it to be him.

136. Who, who knew the circumstances, could remain unmoved?

137. He put his watch in his pocket.

138. Maud wrote very rapidly.

139. Will you permit him and I to stay?

140. Florence is the most beautiful of her sisters.

141. Where was you?

142. Many songs were sung.

143. Him being present, I am happy.

144. The army selected their winter quarters.

145. Rudeness of manners disgust us.

146. One with nine makes ten.

147. Are you sure that it was me?

148. His actions, as well as his speech, were funny.

149. No one knows better than he.

150. Few women are smarter than her.

151. Partnership belongs to that class of business relations in which one or more parties is represented and bound by the acts of another.

152. This is the man whom we think deserved the prize.

153. Their being but a small body, no recognition was given them.

154. He who encounters difficulties at every turn, we should surely pity.

155. Help the poor, disabled soldiers, they who so much need your assistance.

156. Who do you suppose her to be?

157. It matters not whom your companions may be, their influence has its effect upon you.

158. The speaker was not the man whom he seemed to be.

159. If the merchant or his agent indorsed the draft, they should be held responsible.

160. It could not have been him which the speaker intended to reprove.

161. Washington was loved more than any president of the United States.

162. The man who resolves to patiently wait for promotion will surely merit it.

163. Punishing of children is sometimes necessary.

164. The Latin language was spoke by some of our most learned philosophers.

165. I would have spoke sooner, but I did not recognize him.

166. He could never after all his boasting prove nothing.

167. The admission was previously to the trial.

168. Common carriers are bound to transport goods safe.

169. Frank seldom or ever fails to perfectly recite.

170. Among such good friends as you two are no misunderstandings should arise.

171. I passed a man crying with one eye in the street.

172. Who did he refer to in his remarks?

173. Shun him who you know to be two-faced.

174. The effect of him doing that was felt by the entire community.

175. The servant seen the rogue to enter the kitchen.

176. Neither I nor he is prepared to answer.

177. It has recently been discovered that there were coal mines in this vicinity.

178. I know one instance where casting out nines will not disclose the mistakes in addition.

179. Who who knew the parties and their condition could blame them.

180. We gave him the best which we had.

181. This few days lost caused the defeat of the Confederate army.

182. All things which impede my progress shall be removed.

183. Whomsoever will, may be honored by his fellow men.

184. The lady, her who danced so gracefully, will come upon the next train.

185. Washington and Lincoln's administrations were probably the most eventful of any in the history of our nation.

186. The property consists of forty-five acres of which ten is under cultivation.

187. After traveling four days through the woods we went a three days journey across the plains.

188. James' cousin's friend's house is in sight.

189. The man had a short and long cane.

190. The man which owns the farm is my brother.

191. Let some more commoner expression be used.

192. I bought the hat at my friend's Smith's store.

193. The procession at Judge Orton's funeral was very fine and nearly two mlies in length, as was the beautiful prayer of the Rev. Dr. Swing from Chicago.

194. The following verses were written by a young man who has long lain in his grave for his own amusement.

195. A man dug a well with a Roman nose.

196. Either James or John, one of them, will come.

197. Gentlemen's material made up and waited on at their own homes. — *Tailor's Advertisement.*

198. R. C. begs to apologize for not acknowledging P. O. order at the time, but was from home and thus got delayed, misplaced, and forgotten.

199. Lost, a cow belonging to an old woman, with brass knobs on her horns.

200. Lost by a poor lad tied up in a brown paper with a white string a German flute with an overcoat and several other articles of wearing apparel.

APPENDIX.

Under this head we give a number of peculiar sentences, some of which have often caused much comment and discussion.

The student will please bear in mind that the English language is almost, but not quite, a " grammarless tongue," and in disposing of these sentences we have made an attempt to deal with them as we find them, and not as they might have been had our language been constructed upon a model of Greek or Latin.

The pupil will also please remember that there are many expressions in our language the use of which may be sufficiently warranted for conversational style, but at present we would not advise him to engraft them into manuscript.

Notes on Common Expressions.

1. The following expressions are often used in conversational style:

It is me.   That's him.   It is her.

In these sentences the objective forms *me*, *him*, and *her*, are used by *enallage for the subjective forms, *I*, *he*, and *she*.

2. *Angel's footsteps*, *Me* thinks I hear them.

In the above sentence the objective *me* is used by enallage for the subjective form *I*. It is the subject of the verb *thinks*.

Ah *me!*   Dear *me!*

---

* Enallage is the use of one part of speech, or one form for another.

We would not advise the pupil to use the above expressions, but when they are used they seem not altogether unsupported by authority.

Notice the following comments upon them by standard authors:

Careless or inaccurate speakers often use such expressions as, *It is them; It was us; If it were her;* and in the case of IT IS ME, the practice has become so common that it is even regarded as good English by respectable authorities. — *Essentials of Eng. Grammar*, p. 160, *by W. D. Whitney of Yale College.*

Object by enallage; for the nominative in the predicate after an intransitive verb; as, *If I were him; It is me; That's him,* etc.

This use is only warranted in conversational style. — *Holbrook's New Eng. Gram. p.,* 66.

Here *me* is used in the independent case by exclamation.

It is used for the subjective form.

3. In such expressions as, *That nose of yours; That chin of his; etc.*, the words *yours* and *his* are in the objective case. They are used by enallage for the objective forms *you* and *him.*

The use of such sentences as the above is criticised by some grammarians.

4. The following is a list of the most common contractions employed in conversational style: *Can't, don't, isn't, hasn't, haven't, doesn't, couldn't, wouldn't, shouldn't, shan't, *won't*, and aren't.*

† *A'n't* is correctly used for *am not* in the first person singular, but even here it is better to say *I'm not* instead of I *a'n't.*

5. CAN means to be able, to have the power to do or perform a certain act. MAY is used to express liberty or permission.

If you wish to ask permission of me to leave the room, you should not say " *Can I leave the room,*" but " *May I leave the room?*" If you ask me " *Can I leave the room,*" you inquire of me as to your ability to perform this act, but if you ask me " *May I leave the room,*" you are asking my consent to perform this act. We cannot be too careful in the use of these little words.

6. *Peel* or *peeling* means the skin or the rind; as, an apple *peel*; an apple *peeling*. The latter expression is

---

* *Won't* though used for *will not* is properly a contraction of *woll not.*

† *A'n't* is also written *an't* and *ain't.*

sometimes criticised, but *Worcester's Dictionary* has peeling defined thus : *Peeling*, n. *Peel;* skin; hide.

7. The masculine of *laundress* is *laundry-man.* *Seamstress* seems to have no masculine.

8. In regard to the use of the expressions *If I am not mistaken*, and *If I mistake not*, there seems to be no well defined line. According to the strict meaning of the terms there may be a difference in the meaning expressed, but *If I am not mistaken* seems to have sufficient authority to warrant its use even when the speaker wishes to state that he makes a mistake or that he errs.

We quote the following from a standard dictionary : *Mistaken* or *to be mistaken*, is often used in a peculiar manner. In one application, it signifies *to be in error*, or *to be wrong;* but in another application, it signifies *to be misunderstood* or *misconceived;* as, " I am *mistaken*," " He is *mistaken*," i. e. wrong in judgment or opinion : — but, " My opinion, or my remark, is *mistaken;*" implies that I am mistaken, or misunderstood, by my hearers. *Richardson* says, " To be *mistaken* has a twofold applicacation : — " 1. I am *mistaken*, — i. e. *taken*, apprehended, wrongly, erroneously ; I am misapprehended, misunderstood.

" 2. I am *mistaken*, — i. e., *taken*, led, drawn the wrong course or path, astray. I am misled, misguided, betrayed : and consequently I go wrong or astray, I err, I misapprehend." — *Worcester's Dictionary*, p. 918.

9. According to the true meaning of the words which we use, we should say *a sitting hen* and not *a setting hen*.

The simple fact that some one *sets* the hen, does not give us authority to call her *a setting hen.*

The *hen* herself, *sits* and she is a *sitting hen.*

The expression *the setting hen* is probably correct from usage but not otherwise.

We append the following comments from distinguished philologists:

Sitting hen is undoubtedly the right form.— *E. A. Allen, Prof. of English, University of Mo.*

The use of the verb *set* for *sit* in such expressions as, the hen is *setting* on thirteen eggs ; a *setting* hen, etc., although colloquially common, and sometimes tolerated in serious writing, is not to be approved.— *Webster's International Dictionary*, p. 1317.

According to Worcester *the sitting hen* is correct, but according to popular usage *the setting hen* is correct.— *Alfred Holbrook, Pres. National Normal University, Lebanon, O.* ·

Although to speak of a hen as " setting " is far from uncommon, it is by no means good English.— *W. D. Whitney, Prof. of Languages, Yale College.*

10. " You all."

This expression is used in some sections of the country in such a manner that its use has developed into a colloquialism. " You " is either singular or plural, and ordinarily means as much as " you all." When, however, " all " is used after " you " for the sake of emphasis, its use seems to be warranted by sufficient authority to render it perfectly unobjectionable. We append the following comments from Prof. Briggs:

You all seems perfectly good English. *All of you* is equally good. — *L. B. R. Briggs, Prof. of Eng. Harvard University.*

11. Both expressions *To-morrow is Tuesday* and *To-morrow will be Tuesday* seem to be sanctioned by sufficient authority.

We append the following comments from *Butler's Revised Grammar*, p. 240, note 13:

Should we say "To-morrow *is* Wednesday " or " To-morrow *will be* Wednesday? "

As we wish to express an abstract truth rather than a future event, the first form seems preferable. Shakespeare uses this form: " Wednesday *is* to-morrow." — *Romeo and Juliet.* " To-morrow *is* the wedding-day."— *Taming of the shrew.* " *Is* not to-morrow, boy, the ides of March? " — *Julius Cæsar.* " To-morrow *is* the joyful day, Audrey." — *As You Like It.* " To-morrow *is* St. Crispian." — *Henry V.* " To-morrow *is* her birthday." — *Pericles.*

12. In many sentences when the noun is pluralized one of the adjectives may be omitted; as, Read *the* first and *the* second chapter, may also be correctly written: Read the first and second *chapters.*

13. *Says I* and *thinks I* may not be elegant expressions, but when used in such constructions as, *No, no, says I; We agree, says they,* etc., they seem at least to have the sanction of modern usage, and we believe that any one that cares to take the trouble to investigate the Anglo-Saxon language will be convinced that those who are inclined to use the above expressions do not commit such error as some have supposed.

14. With respect to the use of the title *Miss,* when two or more persons of the same name are addressed, there seems to be considerable diversity of opinion. Most grammarians prefer pluralizing the name ; thus : — *The Miss Thompsons; The Miss Bouldins,* but the rules of society seem to favor pluralizing the title ; thus : — *The Misses Thompson; The Misses Bouldin.* It is, perhaps, more nearly in accordance with popular

usage to pluralize the name in conversation and to pluralize the title in composition or in addressing letters. In addressing two or more young ladies of different names the title should be pluralized.

15. MRS. should be pronounced *missis*. We refer those who wish further information on this subject to Webster's and Worcester's Dictionaries.

16. I feel badly.

This expression, although sanctioned by some authorities, would be better thus : " I feel bad." We evidently wish to describe the condition of the subject and to do so should use an adjective and not an adverb. The meaning would be more accurately expressed by the expression : " I am not feeling well."

17. EACH OTHER and ONE ANOTHER. In the use of these expressions *each other* is usually employed when referring to two individuals and *one another* when referring to more than two. Butler says, however, that there is no good authority for these restrictions, and that *each other* and *one another* are applied to either two or more. Johnson says, " To *each* the correspondent is *other* whether it be used of two or a greater number."

18. Mutual Friend. This expression, though subjected to severe criticisms, seems to be very good English, and it is by no means devoid of use among many writers who have won considerable reputation for their careful study of philology. We append the following comments :

Mutual is usually and properly applied to two persons, or their intercourse with each other ; *common* to more than two. *Mutual* friends ; *common* interests or country. — *Worcester's Dictionary*, p. 947.

The use of *mutual* as synonymous with *common* is

inconsistent with the idea of interchange, or reciprocal relation, which properly belongs to it; but the word has been so used by many *writers of high authority.* The present tendency is toward a careful discrimination.— *Webster's International Dictionary*, p. 958.

I think *mutual friend* is sanctioned by Webster's new Dictionary with some reserve.— *Noah Porter, LL.D., Pres. of Yale College.*

19. **Goose**, meaning a tailor's smoothing iron, seems to have no plural, and when it is necessary to use the plural, according to Dr. Noah Porter it may be written *smoothing irons.*

20. **Complexioned.** Do not say *she is dark complected*, or *he is light complected.*

The proper expressions are, *She is dark complexioned,* or *He is light complexioned.*

21. The "*ed*" should be accented in the following words, when used as adjectives, namely; *Beloved, cursed, aged, learned,* and *winged,* and should be marked with the grave accent, thus *Learnèd.*

It was once accented in many other words, but all except the above named have been changed.

22. **Betwixt** and **between** strictly speaking apply to two objects only. But in many instances they may be correctly used when reference is made to a number of things, as the following sentences will illustrate:

"A choice *between* two or more alternatives." — *Mulligan.* "*Betwixt* the slender boughs came glimpses of her ivory neck." — *Bryant.* "*Between* two or more authors different readers will differ." — *Campbell.*

23. **Either** is properly used for one of two things, but it is often used in the sense of *anyone* to mean one of

several; as, If from a point within a triangle two straight lines are drawn to the extremities of *either* side, etc. — *Loomis's Geom., Bk. 1, Prop. IX.*

Scarce a palm of ground could be gotten by *either* of the *three.* — *Bacon.* There have been *three* famous talkers in Great Britain, *either* of whom would illustrate what I say about dogmatists. — *Holmes.*

Few writers hesitate to use *either* in what is called a triple alternative; such as, We must *either* stay where we are, proceed, or recede.— *Latham.* *Either* is sometimes used in the sense of *each* to indicate both of two; as, His flowing hair in curls on *either* cheek played.— *Milton.*

On *either* side . . . was there the tree of life.— *Rev.* XXII., 2.

24. **Neither** by strict meaning applies to one of two objects only; yet, Dr. Webster says, that by usage it is applicable to any number referring to individuals separately considered.

25. We are glad to notice that at present the tendency is to drop the hyphen from compound words in general use. We can give no definite rules as to when the hyphen should be used and when it should be omitted; the only way to learn this is by consulting the latest dictionary whenever you are the least doubtful. The following are a few compound words in which the hyphen has recently been omitted: *bookkeeping, shorthand, typewriting, typewriter, schoolboy, schoolgirl, schoolhouse, schoolmaster, schoolmate, doorcase, doorkeeper, doorway, doornail, doorplate, bookbinder, bookkeeper, bookmark, bookcase, bookseller, toothbrush, toothpick, bedtime, clothesline, clothespress, woodwork, woolgrower, billhead, airpump, airhole, bareheaded,*

grapevine, homemade, hotbed, birdcage, blackmail, blacksnake, coffeehouse, coffeepot, courtyard, dogday, footprint, football, forcepump, fishhook, flagstaff, bloodhound, flytrap.

26. **Please.** Such sentences as, *Please excuse me,* and *Please bring me a glass of water,* are sanctioned by good authority, notwithstanding the fact that many contend that the sign "to" is improperly omitted before the infinitive, and that they should be, *Please to excuse me,* and *Please to bring me a glass of water.*

27. The expressions *4 times 5 are 20,* and *4 times 5 is 20,* are both warranted by sufficient authority.

When expanded they read: 4 taken to the extent of 5 times is 20, or 4 times of 5 are 20.

28. Such expressions as, *You had better go, You had better stay, etc.,* are warranted by good usage. It would be more in harmony with the rules of grammar, however, to use *would* instead of *had.*

29. The plural number and the possessive singular of letters, figures, and characters, are alike in form, both being formed by the annexation of the *'s* thus, plural 4's possessive, singular, 4's.

The possessive plural is formed by annexing an apostrophe to the plural, thus 4's'.

30. It is more elegant to say *the train had left before we arrived,* than to say, *the train left before we arrived.*

Had left expresses time more remote than expressed by *left.* Thus making it a better verb to use in the sentence with arrived.

31. The word *whether* implies a selection, and should not be used for if after the verbs *doubt, fear, etc.* I

doubt *whether* he will come, should be, I doubt *if* he will come.

32. **Farther** and **further.** In the use of these words many contend that *further* should be used when something additional is meant, and that *farther* should be used when referring to distance. This distinction, however, is not usually observed and it seems to make but little difference which form is used. It may not be the best usage to write *If you desire any farther information*, but *further* may certainly be correctly used when referring to something additional or to distance.

33. *Their* is sometimes used to represent nouns or pronouns in the singular connected by *or* or *nor;* as, Not on outward claims could he or she build *their* pretensions to please.

No boy or girl should whisper to *their* neighbor. In these sentences the pronoun does not agree with its antecedent in number, but Mr. Harvey among others has sanctioned its use.

34. The expression *that far*, although used for *so far*, seems to have the sanction of, at least, popular usage. *That* when used in such expressions as the above is an adverb.

35. When two or more nouns are connected so as to denote but one thing they should have the same form of verb as a singular noun ; as, *A hue and cry was raised; Bread and butter is excellent food*.

36. **Hanged** is preferable to *hung* when reference is had to death or execution by suspension, and it is more common; but in instances other than this *hung* seems to be the form most commonly employed.

37. Henry's and John's books. With regard to writing such expressions as this, there seems to be no generally accepted method, and when we wish to speak of two books one of which belongs to Henry and the other to John, it may be written *Henry's and John's books* or *Henry's and John's book*.

We call attention to the following comments from two grammarians of, perhaps, equal ability, but antithetic opinions:

If a noun is made plural when it is expressed, it will also be plural when it is implied. It is good English to say, " A *father's* or *mother's sisters* are aunts;" but the meaning is " A father's *sisters* or a mother's *sisters* are aunts."

But a recent school critic teaches differently, thus: " When different things of the same name belong to different possessors, the sign should be annexed to each; as *Adams', Davies',* and *Perkins' Arithmetics;* i. e., *three different books.*" Here the example is fictitious, and has almost as many errors as words. It would be much better English to say, " *Adams's, Davies's,* and *Perkins's Arithmetic. — Goold Brown's Gram. of Eng. Grammars,* p. 510.

Goold Brown and others maintain that such expressions as " Johnson's and Richardson's *Dictionaries* " are incorrect, because we cannot say, " Johnson's *Dictionaries* and Richardson's *Dictionaries.*" Of course we do not say, " *Johnson's Dictionaries,*" for the very good reason that we are thinking of but *one* thing; but we do say, " Johnson's and Richardson's *Dictionaries* for the equally good reason that we are thinking of *two* things. We say, " The Old and New Testaments, because we are thinking of two Testaments. A person holding in his hand a knife belonging to John and another knife belonging to William would hardly venture to say, "These are John's and William's knife," even though he might have Brown's Grammar of English Grammars open before him.

The attempt to better the English by using the form "Johnson's Dictionary and Richardson's" is a failure; for this form is stiff and pedantic. A speaker may say, "I have consulted Johnson's Dictionary," and then add, "and Richardson's," as the result of a second thought; but if he sets out to mention both, this form is contrary to the English idiom.— *Butler's Revised Grammar*, p. 188.

38. *Each of you shall have your money.*

Your in this sentence should be *his*. The antecedent of the pronoun *your* is *each* and not *you*.

39. *Reared* seems to be preferable to *raised* when speaking of *persons* and, perhaps, the reverse is true when speaking of *live stock*; as, *He* was *reared* in Missouri; Those *cattle* were *raised* in Texas.

In some parts of the United States *raised* is commonly applied to *rearing* or *bringing up* children: as, "I was *raised*, as they say in Virginia, among the mountains of the North."— *Paulding.* "In the place in which he was *raised.*"— *Jefferson.*

40. In such expressions as *the then ministry* and *the above discourse*, the words *then* and *above* are adjectives. These expressions, though sometimes criticised, seem to be good English.

IRREGULAR VERBS.

The following list of irregular verbs has been prepared with great care, and strictly in accordance with

the usages laid down in Webster's International Dictionary. When a verb has more than one form for its past
tense and perfect participle we have written the forms
in the order in which they are preferred.

List of Irregular Verbs.

PRESENT.	PAST.	PAST PART.
Abide,	abode,	abode,
Am or be,	was,	been,
Arise,	arose,	arisen.
Awake,	awoke or awaked,	awaked or awoke.
Bear,	bore or bare,	born.
Bear,	bore or bare,	borne.
Beat,	beat,	beat or beaten.
Become,	became,	become.
Befall,	befell,	befallen.
Beget,	begot,	begot or begotten.
Begin,	began or begun,	began or begun.
Begird,	begirt or begirded,	begirt.
Behold,	beheld,	beheld.
Belay,	belaid or belayed,	belaid or belayed.
Bend,	bended or bent,	bended or bent.
Bereave,	bereaved or bereft,	bereaved or bereft.
Beseech,	besought,	besought.
Beset,	beset,	beset.
Bespeak,	bespoke,	bespoke or bespoken.
Bespit,	bespit,	bespit or bespitten.
Bespread,	bespread,	bespread.
Bestrew,	bestrewed,	bestrewed or bestrown.
Bestick,	bestuck,	bestuck.
Bestride,	bestrode,	bestridden, bestride or bestrode.
Bet,	bet or betted,	bet or betted.
Betake,	betook,	betaken.

PRESENT.	PAST.	PAST PART.
Bethink,	bethought,	bethought.
Bethump,	bethumped or bethumpt,	bethumped or bethumpt.
Beweep,	bewept,	bewept.
Bid,	bade or bid,	bidden or bid.
Bind,	bound,	bound.
Bite,	bit,	bitten or bit.
Bleed,	bled,	bled.
Blend,	blended or blent,	blended or blent.
Bless,	blessed or blest,	blessed or blest.
Blow,	blew,	blown.
Break,	broke,	broken.
Breed,	bred,	bred.
Bring,	brought,	brought.
Build,	built,	built.
Burn,	burned or burnt,	burned or burnt.
Burst,	burst,	burst.
Buy,	bought,	bought.
Cast,	cast,	cast.
Catch,	caught or catched,	caught or catched.
Chide,	chid,	chidden or chid.
Choose,	chose,	chosen.
Cleave,	cleft,	cleft, cleaved or cloven.
Cling,	clung,	clung.
Clothe,	clothed or clad,	clothed or clad.
Come,	came,	come.
Cost,	cost,	cost.
Creep,	crept,	crept.
Crow,	crew or crowed,	crowed.
Curse,	cursed or curst,	cursed o r curst.
Cut,	cut,	cut.
Dare,	durst or dared,	dared.

PRESENT.	PAST.	PAST PART.
Deal,	dealt,	dealt.
Dig,	dug or digged,	dug or digged.
Dive,	dived or dove,	dived or dove.
Do,	did,	done.
Draw,	drew,	drawn.
Dream,	dreamed or dreamt,	dreamed or dreamt.
Dress,	dressed or drest,	dressed or drest.
Drink,	drank,	drunk or drunken.
Drive,	drove,	driven.
Dwell,	dwelled or dwelt,	dwelled or dwelt.
Eat,	ate,	eaten.
Engird,	engirded or engirt,	engirded or engirt.
Engrave,	engraved,	engraved or engraven.
Fall,	fell,	fallen.
Feed,	fed,	fed.
Feel,	felt,	felt.
Fight,	fought,	fought.
Find,	found,	found.
Flee,	fled,	fled.
Fling,	flung,	flung.
Fly,	flew,	flown.
Forbear,	forbore,	forborne.
Forget,	forgot,	forgotten or forgot.
Forgive,	forgave,	forgiven.
Forsake,	forsook,	forsaken.
Freeze,	froze,	frozen.
Geld,	gelded or gelt,	gelded or gelt.
Get,	got,	got.
Gild,	gilded or gilt,	gilded or gilt.
Gird,	girt or girded,	girt or girded.
Give,	gave,	given.
Go,	went,	gone.
Grave,	graved,	graven or graved.

PRESENT.	PAST.	PAST PART.
Grind,	ground,	ground.
Grow,	grew,	grown.
Hang,	hanged or hung,	hanged or hung.
Have,	had,	had.
Hear,	heard,	heard.
Heave,	heaved or hove,	heaved, hove or hoven.
Hew,	hewed,	hewed or hewn.
Hide,	hid,	hidden or hid.
Hit,	hit,	hit.
Hold,	held,	held.
Hurt,	hurt,	hurt.
Keep,	kept,	kept.
Kneel,	knelt or kneeled,	knelt or kneeled.
Knit,	knit or knitted,	knit or knitted.
Know,	knew,	known,
Lade,	laded,	laded or laden.
Lay,	laid,	laid.
Lead,	led,	led.
Lean,	leaned or leant.	leaned or leant.
Leap,	leaped or leapt,	leaped or leapt.
Learn,	learned or learnt,	learned or learnt.
Leave,	left,	left.
Lend,	lent,	lent.
Let,	let,	let.
Lie,	lay,	lain.
Lie,	lied,	lied.
Light,	lighted or lit,	lighted or lit.
Lose,	lost,	lost.
Make,	made,	made.
Mean,	meant,	meant.
Meet,	met,	met.
Misgive,	misgave,	misgiven.
Mislead,	misled,	misled.

PRESENT.	PAST.	PAST PART.
Misspend,	misspent,	misspent.
Mow	mowed,	mowed or mown.
Outdo,	outdid,	outdone.
Pay,	paid,	paid.
Pen,	penned or pent,	penned or pent.
Put,	put,	put.
Quit,	quit or quitted,	quit or quitted.
Rap,	rapped or rapt,	rapped or rapt.
Read,	read,	read.
Reave,	reaved or reft,	reaved or reft.
Rend,	rent,	rent.
Repay,	repaid,	repaid.
Rid,	rid or ridded,	rid or ridded.
Ride,	rode,	ridden.
Ring,	rang or rung,	rung.
Rise,	rose,	risen.
Rive,	rived,	rived or riven.
Run,	ran or run,	run.
Saw,	sawed,	sawed or sawn.
Say,	said,	said.
See,	saw,	seen.
Seek,	sought,	sought.
Seethe,	seethed,	seethed or sodden.
Sell,	sold,	sold.
Send,	sent,	sent.
Set,	set,	set.
Shake,	shook,	shaken.
Shape,	shaped,	shaped or shapen.
Shave,	shaved,	shaved or shaven.
Shear,	sheared or shore,	sheared or shorn.
Shed,	shed,	shed.
Shine,	shone,	shone.
Shoe,	shod,	shod.

PRESENT.	PAST.	PAST PART.
Shoot,	shot,	shot.
Show,	showed,	shown or showed.
Shred,	shred or shredded,	shred or shredded.
Shrink,	shrank or shrunk,	shrunk or shrunken.
Shut,	shut,	shut.
Sing,	sung or sang,	sung.
Sink,	sunk or sank,	sunk.
Sit,	sat,	sat.
Slay,	slew,	slain.
Sleep,	slept,	slept.
Slide,	slid,	slidden or slid.
Sling,	slung,	slung.
Slink,	slunk,	slunk.
Slit,	slit or slitted,	slit or slitted.
Smell,	smelled or smelt,	smelled or smelt.
Smite,	smote,	smitten.
Sow,	sowed,	sown or sowed.
Speak,	spoke,	spoken.
Speed,	sped or speeded,	sped or speeded.
Spell,	spelled or spelt,	spelled or spelt.
Spend,	spent,	spent.
Spill,	spilled or spilt,	spilled or spilt.
Spin,	spun,	spun,
Spit,	spit,	spit.
Split,	split or splitted,	split or splitted.
Spoil,	spoiled or spoilt,	spoiled or spoilt.
Spread,	spread,	spread.
Spring,	sprang or sprung,	sprung.
Stand,	stood,	stood.
Stave,	staved or stove,	staved or stove.
Stay,	stayed or staid,	stayed or staid.
Steal,	stole,	stolen.
Stick,	stuck,	stuck.

PRESENT.	PAST.	PAST PART.
Sting,	stung,	stung.
Stink,	stunk or stank,	stunk.
Strew,	strewed,	strewed or strewn.
Stride,	strode,	stridden.
Strike,	struck,	struck or stricken.
String,	strung,	strung or stringed.
Strive,	strove,	striven or strove.
Strow,	strowed,	strown or strowed.
Swear,	swore,	sworn.
Sweat,	sweat or sweated,	sweat or sweated.
Sweep,	swept,	swept.
Swell,	swelled,	swelled or swollen.
Swim,	swam or swum,	swum.
Swing,	swung,	swung.
Take,	took,	taken.
Teach,	taught,	taught.
Tear,	tore,	torn.
Tell,	told,	told.
Think,	thought,	thought.
Thrive,	throve or thrived,	thrived or thriven
Throw,	threw,	thrown.
Thrust,	thrust,	thrust.
Tread,	trod,	trodden or trod.
Unbind,	unbound,	unbound.
Undo,	undid,	undone.
Wake,	waked or woke,	waked or woke.
Wear,	wore,	worn.
Weave,	wove or weaved,	woven, wove or weaved.
Wed,	wedded,	wedded or wed.
Weep,	wept,	wept.
Wet,	wet or wetted,	wet or wetted.
Win,	won,	won,

PRESENT.	PAST.	PAST PART.
Wind,	wound or winded,	wound or winded.
Withhold,	withheld,	withheld.
Withstand,	withstood,	withstood.
Wont,	wont,	wont or wonted.
Work,	worked or wrought,	worked or wrought.
Wreathe,	wreathed,	wreathed or wreathen.
Wring,	wrung,	wrung.
Write,	wrote,	written.

EXERCISES.

The pupil will criticise the following sentences, making corrections when necessary.

Many of them will be found to be correct according to some authorities and incorrect according to others. Some of them are correct or incorrect according to the idea intended to be conveyed and are simply placed here for the purpose of calling attention to them.

1. They had better go home.
2. Please give me a drink.
3. I have a nice compliment for you.
4. Read the four first stanzas of the poem.
5. I never thought of him going to town.
6. This will do equally as well.
7. Can I leave my seat for a few minutes?
8. Her and I can carry it easy enough.
9. I heard it from our mutual friend.
10. Read slower if you please.
11. He was presented a book.
12. Two many orators are in the audience for only to too speak.
13. I dare say she is as old, if not older than you.
14. Actions speak plainer than words.

15. The house was divided on the question.

16. Bread and butter is good.

17. He acted rather strange this morning.

18. Laura was given a bouquet.

19. The hawk caught the pigeon while it was flying.

20. The boy has a new pair of boots.

21. He talks like you do.

22. Shall you speak to him or I?

23. He poured oil on and burned the house.

24. Lettie, please shut the door.

25. It was much easier done than we expected.

26. The prisoner was sorry he ran away five minutes after he escaped.

27. The little girl ran over the bed with flowers on.

28. Don't say nothing about it.

29. It is pleasanter to-day than it was yesterday.

30. Pleasure and not books occupy his mind.

31. Blanche was very beautiful which caused her to have many admirers.

32. Them that study grammar, talk no better than me.

33. I do not know but what he is right.

34. My head feels badly.

35. The soil is adapted for hemp and tobacco. -

36. What is the matter of him.

37. I differ from you in the opinion you just expressed.

38. He fought in the Revolution.

39. They are hard to work.

40. You can confide on him.

41. That class of pupils are diligent.

42. They that honor me, I will honor.

43. Either you or I are greatly mistaken in our judgment.

44. The field yielded about twenty bushel to the acre.

45. Tell me whom it was.

46. Go and lay down.

47. I came in the room and set down.

48. His constitution, as well as his fortune, require care.

49. The public are invited to attend.

50. Columbus knew that the earth was round.

51. He said to me, who is you?

52. Try to get well as quick as you can.

53. The fleet were soon out of sight.

54. They look quite as well as us.

55. One or both of the girls has gone to the party.

56. Let you and I endeavor to restrain him.

57. It couldn't have been them that we passed.

58. She is as good, if not better than he.

59. He gave me too much.

60. I don't think he has come yet.

61. It was believed to be her.

62. I remember it being done.

63. The number of senators are limited to two.

64. I shall proceed no further.

65. They have gotten back.

66. He has forgot his hat.

67. He dove after the lost pulley.

68. The lamp has been lit.

69. They have rang the bell.

70. She sung a song.

71. The ship sank.

72. The melons have shrunken until they are quite small.

73. They slayed their brother.

74. They swang an hour.

75. He swum across the creek.

76. They have drank the water.

77. They throwed him overboard.

78. He thrusted his hand in the bag.

79. The boiler bursted yesterday.

80. She smelt the rose.

81. From memory he spinned the thread of fancy.

82. Wanted, a room for a single gentleman, twelve feet long and six feet wide.

83. A child was run over by a heavy wagon, four years old, wearing a short pink dress, and bronze boots, whose parents are not yet found.

84. I would like the congregation to be seated, as I wish to say a few words, before I begin.

85. I cannot think of leaving you without distress.

86. Mr. French needs a surgeon, who has broken his arm.

87. He needs no spectacles, that cannot see; nor boots, that cannot walk.

88. Found, a white-handled knife, by a child, that has a broken back.

89. A man walked down the street, followed by a little dog, sporting a green neck-tie and patent leather boots.

90. The man who sat writing with a Roman nose was ordered to leave the room.

91. An extensive view is presented from the fourth story of the Delaware River.

92. Wanted a groom to take charge of two horses of a serious turn of mind.

NOTES ON ANALYSIS OF SENTENCES.

1. *John is a friend of mine.* The word *mine* in this sentence may be disposed of as a possessive pronoun modifying *friends* understood.

2. Adverbs sometimes modify prepositional phrases as will be seen from the following sentence: We walked

nearly across the bridge. Here it is evident that *nearly* modifies the prepositional phrase *across the bridge*.

3. *Before Abraham was I am.* Mr. Webster says, that in the above sentence *before* is a preposition; if such be the case, the clause, *Abraham was* is certainly the object.

We think, however, that it would be better to dispose of *before* as a conjunctive adverb, modifying *was* and connecting the subordinate clause *Abraham was* to *am*.

4. *He came running.* In this sentence *running* is an adjective used as an attribute. It may also be disposed of as an adverb.

5. *As* is frequently used as a preposition, as, He went *as* an ambassador. That is, He went, *in the capacity of* an ambassador.

6. *He died ten years ago.* *Ago* in this sentence is an adjective, modifying the noun *years*. It may also be disposed of as an adverb modifying *died*.

7. *He came just as I left.* In this sentence *just* is an adverb modifying the conjunctive adverb *as*.

8. *There is no fireside howsoe'er defended but has one vacant chair.* Mr. Swinton says, that *but* in the above sentence is a conjunctive, or relative, pronoun.

9. *Worth* is usually considered an adjective, in such sentences as, The hat is *worth* five dollars. But many grammarians class it as a preposition. Mr. Worcester says, that *worth* has the construction of a preposition, as it admits of the objective case after it, without an intervening preposition.

10. *But that.* What rests, *but that* the mortal sentence pass. *But* in this sentence is given by Mr. Goold Brown as a preposition, having the clause " that the mortal sentence pass " for its object.

But that may also be disposed of as a subordinate conjunction.

11. *He must needs go.* In this sentence *needs* is an adverb. The expression is equivalent to, He must *of necessity* go.

12. *That book is hers.* In the above sentence *hers* is a pronoun limiting the noun *book* understood. The possessives in such sentences as, *that knife is his; that house is theirs*, etc., may be disposed of in a similar manner.

13. *Many a, such a,* etc., are commonly regarded as adjective phrases ; as, He received *many a* warning, but he disregarded them all.

14. *Who,* in such sentences as, *I know who took the book,* is certainly not a conjunctive pronoun as many grammarians have supposed, but the clause " who took the book " is evidently the object of the verb *know.* Mr. Holbrook says, in discussing this question in the sentence, " I learned many years ago *who was the first President,"* I did not intend to say that I learned George Washington, who was, etc., but I learned (how to answer the question) who was the first president. We think that in such sentences as the above *who* is simply a pure pronoun without any of the connective qualities possessed by the conjunctive pronoun.

In the following sentence, " I heard *who did it,"* the meaning certainly is not, " I heard the person who did it," but that the clause " who did it," is the plain object of the verb *heard.*

15. In such expressions as, *freezing cold, scalding hot, dripping wet,* etc., the words *freezing, scalding, dripping,* are adverbs modifying the adjectives following them.

16. *They love each other.* Some adjectives when used, as nouns, are frequently in apposition with a plural noun as the above sentence illustrates ; the word *each* being in apposition with *they.*

Some grammarians contend that an ellipsis should be supplied thus ; They love : each loves the other.

The same disposition may be made of such sentences as, *They loved one another.*

17. *Like, near and nigh.* A preposition is usually supplied after the above words in such sentences as, *He looks like* (unto) *you; He sat near* (to) *the wall;* but there is no necessity for doing so as the better disposition of the words *like, nigh,* etc., is to regard them as prepositions having the nouns and pronouns following as their objects.

18. Such expressions as, *He is gone, The race is run, All are departed, He is come, etc.,* though criticised by some, are, nevertheless, good English.

There seems to be a shade of difference in the meaning expressed by *He is gone,* and *he has gone.*

Words Variously Used.

1. **A.** (1) **Adj.,** "*A* horse;" "*An* ounce." (2) **Prep.,** "He went *a* hunting."

2. **About.** (1) **Adv.,** "They run *about.*" (2) **Prep.,** "He spoke *about* John.."

3. **Above.** (1) **Adv.,** "They stand *above.*" (2) **Prep.,** "They stand *above* the throng." (3) **Noun,** "They hail from *above.*"

4. **Adieu.** (1) **Noun,** "He said *adieu.*" (2) **Interjection,** "*Adieu!* my friend."

5. **After.** (1) **Adv.,** "He died soon *after.*" (2) **Prep.,** "We sent him *after* James." (3) **Conj. Adv.,** "He studied *after* you left."

6. **Again.** (1) **Adv.,** "Say that *again.*"

7. **Alike.** (1) **Adj.,** "Those horses are *alike.*" (2) **Adv.,** "He is *alike* unlearned and unloved."

8. **All.** (1) **Noun,** "Take my *all;* it is yours."

(2) **Adj.**, "*All* things are ready." (3) **Adv.**, "It is *all* gone."

9. **Any.** (1) **Adj.**, "Have you *any* money?" (2) **Adv.**, "They are not *any* wiser than we."

10. **As.** (1) **Adv.**, "He is *as* good as she." (2) **Conj. Adv.**, "Go *as* they go." (3) **Sub. Conj.**, "*As* we sow, so shall we reap." (4) **Conj. Pro.**, "Such *as* I have I give unto thee." (5) **Prep.**, "He went *as* an ambassador."

11. **Before.** (1) **Adv.**, "They came *before*." (2) **Prep.**, "A long road lies *before* us." (3) **Conj. Adv.**, "He came *before* you left."

12. **Below.** (1) **Noun**, "We walked from *below*." (2) **Adj.**, "He is one of the hands *below*." (3) **Adv.**, "They went *below*." (4) **Prep.**, "The water is *below* the rock."

13. **Best.** (1) **Noun**, "Let us do our *best*." (2) **Adj.**, "These are the *best* peaches." (3) **Adv.**, "We can *best* agree at present."

14. **Better.** (1) **Noun**, "Respect your *betters*." (2) **Verb.**, "Time *betters* time." (3) **Adj.**, "The old man is the *better* lawyer." (4) **Adv.**, "He is loved *better* now."

15. **Both.** (1) **Adj.**, "Listen to *both* stories." (2) **Co-ordinate Conj.**, "She is *both* fair and frail."

16. **But.** (1) **Adv.**, "If the boat sinks, we shall *but* drown." (2) **Prep.**, "All *but* him had fled." (3) **Part of Comp. Prep.**, "He would starve *but* for his family." (4) **Co-ordinate Conj.**, "James went, *but* John stayed.

17. **By.** (1) **Adv.**, "They drove *by* in the surrey." (2) **Prep.**, "The book came *by* mail."

18. **Close.** (1) **Adj.**, "They are *close*, stingy men." (2) **Adv.**, "They followed *close* upon us."

19. **Else.** (1) **Adj.**, "Offend no one *else*." (2) **Adv.**, "How *else* could that be done?" (3) **Co-ordinate Conj.**, "You do not like me, *else* would I go."

20. **Enough.** (1) **Noun**, "We gave him *enough*." (2) **Adj.**, "I have money *enough*." (3) **Adv.**, "I have known you long *enough*."

21. **Except.** (1) **Prep.**, "He studies nothing *except* grammar." (2) **Sub. Conj.**, "*Except* ye repent ye shall all likewise perish."

22. **Far.** (1) **Noun**, "They came from *afar*." (2) **Adj.**, "He came from a *far* country." (3) **Adv.**, "He is *far* away."

23. **Farewell.** (1) **Noun**, "He said a last *farewell*." (2) **Adj.**, "A *farewell* entertainment was given her." (3) **Interj.**, "Farewell."

24. **Fast.** **Noun**, "The annual *fast* was observed." (2) **Verb**, "They did *fast* four days." (3) **Adj.**, "He is a *fast* horse." (4) **Adv.**, "He talks *fast*."

25. **Few.** (i) **Noun**, "A *few* were there." (2) **Adj.**, "I have a *few* letters to write."

26. **For.** (1) **Prep.**, "They looked *for* him." (2) **Sub. Conj.**, "I am going home; *for* it is raining."

27. **Full.** (1) **Noun**, "We will return at *full* of tide." (2) **Verb**, "The moon *fulls* to-night." (3) **Adj.**, "The pail is *full*." (4) **Adv.**, "They laughed *full* well."

28. **Hard.** (1) **Adj.**, "This is a *hard* task." (2) **Adv.**, "The house stood *hard* by."

29. **However.** (1) **Adv.**, "Death spares none, *however* powerful." (2) **Introductory Conj,**, "*However*, you need not go."

30. **Ill.** (1) **Noun**, "The *ills* of life are many." (2) **Adj.**, "They are *ill*." (3) **Adv.**, "*Ill* fares the man."

31. **Indeed.** (1) **Adv.**, "He is *indeed* lame." (2) **Introductory Conj.**, "*Indeed* you shall not go."

32. **Late.** (1) **Adj.**, "A *late* train caused the delay." (2) **Adv.**, "He came *late*."

33. **Like.** (1) **Noun,** "*Like* begets *like*." (2) **Verb,** "I *like* you." (3) **Adj.**, "They had *like* opportunities." (4) **Prep.**, "He talked *like* a maniac."

34. **Low.** (1) **Adj.**, "This bough is *low*." (2) **Adv.**, "He sang *low*."

35. **More.** (1) **Noun,** "They had no *more*." (2) **Adj.**, "*More* men are coming." (3) **Adv.**, "He is *more* truthful."

36. **Much.** (1) **Noun,** "We made *much* of him." (2) **Adj.**, "He is credited with *much* wisdom." (3) **Adv.**, "Read *much*, think more."

37. **Nay.** (1) **Noun,** "The *nays* have it." (2) **Adv.**, "*Nay*, we believe it not."

38. **No.** (1) **Noun,** "The *noes* have it." (2) **Adj.**, "He has *no* home." (3) **Adv.**, "I can go *no* farther."

39. **Notwithstanding.** (1) **Prep.**, "We went *notwithstanding* the weather." (2) **Sub. Conj.**, "He is rude *notwithstanding* he is educated."

40. **Now.** (1) **Noun,** Eternity is a never ending *now*." (2) **Adv.**, "Let us go *now*."

41. **Once.** (1) **Noun,** "*Once* is enough." (2) **Adv.**, "He went with us *once*."

42. **Only.** (1) **Adj.**, "This is the *only* book." (2) **Adv.**, "I read *only*, I do not play."

43. **Over.** (1) **Adv.**, "The play is *over*." (2) **Prep.**, "We drove *over* the grass."

44. **Right.** (1) **Noun,** *Right* makes might." (2) **Adj.**, "He is *right*." (3) **Adv.**, "You should be *right* sorry for that."

45. Save. (1) Verb, *Save* your money." (2) Prep., " They all went, *save* one."

46. So. (1) Adv., " He is *so* good." (2) Sub. Conj., " As we sow *so* shall we reap."

47. That (1) Adj., " *That* man is mean." (2) Conj. Pron., " Ye *that* hear my words, heed them." (3) Expletive, " He heard *that* they had gone." (4) Sub. Conj., " He gazed so long *that* both his eyes were dazzled." (5) Adv., " Now *that* (when) all women of condition are well educated we hear no more of these apprehensions."

48. The. (1) Adj., " *The* moon is shining." (2) Adv., " *The* harder we study the more we learn."

49. Then. (1) Noun, "Many changes may take place between now and *then*." (2) Adv., " He *then* went to the house." (3) Sub. Conj., " If you can not use it, *then* do not take it."

50. There. (1) Adv., " He boards *there*." (2) Expletive, "*There* was a man named John."

51. Till. (1) Noun, " The *till* contains money." (2) Verb, " They *till* the ground." (3) Prep., "He stayed *till* Tuesday." (4) Conj. Adv., " Do not go *till* he returns."

52. Up. (1) Noun, " Our *ups* and downs affect only us." (2) Adv., " They are going *up*." (3) Prep., " He ran *up* the hill."

53. Well. (1) Noun, "The *well* is an old one." (2) Verb, " Sweet sounds *well* up from below." (3) Adj., "All is *well*." (4) Adv., " The task was *well* done." (5) Introductory Adv., " *Well*, where are you going."

54. What. (1) Pron., " Say *what* you think." (2) Adj., " *What* house is that." (3) Adv., " *What* by industry and *what* by economy he amassed a fortune." (4) Interj., " *What!* are you going to leave us? "

11

55. When. (1) **Adv.**, " *When* did he come." (2) **Conj. Adv.**, " Write *when* you reach home."

56. Which. (1) **Conj. Pron.**, " This is the book in *which* it is found." (2) **Adj.**, "*Which* horse did he buy?"

57. While. (1) **Noun**, " Is it worth *while?* " (2) **Verb**, " He *whiles* away his time." (3) **Conj. Adv.**, " They stood uncovered *while* he prayed."

58. Worse. (1) **Noun**, " We take this for better or for *worse*." (3) **Adv.**, " He acted *worse*."

59. Worth. (1) **Noun**, " *Worth* makes the man." (2) **Verb**, " Woe *worth* the day." **Adj.**, " She is *worth* ten thousand."

60. Yet. (1) **Adv.**, " The house *yet* stands." **Co-ordinate Conj.**, " He is a smuggler, *yet* will I trust him."

61. Yonder. (1) **Adj.**, "*Yonder* hill is just in sight." (2) **Adv.**, " Who stands *yonder?* "

EXERCISES FOR ANALYSIS.

1. Whom the shoe fits let him put it on.
2. The heights by great men reached and kept
   Were not attained by sudden flight,
   But they while their companions slept
   Were toiling upward in the night.
3. He fell full length on the floor.
4. I take my soup hot.
5. Full well they laughed with counterfeited glee
   At all his jokes, for many a joke had he,
   Full well the busy whisper, circling round,
   Conveyed the dismal tidings when he frowned.
6. There is beauty in that letter
   Which my sister wrote to me.

No hand can trace one better —
More easy, plain, and free.
7. A mariner whom fate compelled
To make his home ashore,
Lived in yon cottage on the mount,
With ivy mantled o'er.
8. Vast commerce, with her busy hum of men,
Owes to the sword less homage than the pen.
9. Count that day lost, whose low descending sun
Views at thy hand, no worthy action done.
10. Lovers are blind and cannot see the petty follies
that themselves commit.
11. Immodest words admit of no defense;
For lack of decency is lack of sense.
12. The piper loud and louder blew,
The dancers quick and quicker flew.
13. Beneath this stone my wife doth lie;
She's now at rest and so am I.
14. In pride, in reasoning pride, our error lies,
All quit their spheres and rush into the skies.
15. Be not the first by whom the new are tried,
Nor yet the last to lay the old aside.
16. Ring out a slowly dying cause,
And ancient forms of party strife,
Ring in the nobler modes of life.
17. The Indians had no written language but they had
ways of giving information to one another by signs on
rocks and trees, they had no money, but for coins used
wampum beads.
18. John declared it seemed to be impossible for him
to tell what words are double relatives and what are
interrogative pronominal adjectives.
19. Misses, the tale that I relate
This lesson seems to carry.

Choose not alone a proper mate,
But a proper time to marry.
20. There is a pleasure in the pathless woods
There is a rapture on the lonely shore.
There is society where none intrudes
By the deep sea and music in its roar.

WORDS DISCRIMINATED.

Below we have given a short list of common words
and discriminated the uses thereof. This list should be
studied carefully, as nothing is more calculated to inspire
confidence in one's ability than a nice choice of words.
The pupil should be required to compose original sentences illustrating the proper use of each of these words.

Admittance, Admission.

It would probably be quite difficult to draw a definite
line between the uses of these words, though *admittance*
is now chiefly confined to its primary sense of access
into some locality or building. Thus we write on the
doors of shops, etc., " No admittance." We speak of
admittance to public places of entertainment, and of *admission* of irregularities, rights, etc. When we speak of
admission to a public entertainment the meaning is not
quite that of *admittance* within the walls of the building,
but rather a reception into the audience, or access to the
performance or entertainment, as the case may be.

Assurance never failed to get *admittance* into the house
of the great. — Moore.

The gospel has then only a free *admission* into the
assent of the understanding. — South.

Effect, Affect.

Effect is that which is produced by a cause. Whatever is *effected* is always the consequence of a specific design. It requires a rational agent to *effect*.

Affect, according to its literal sense, means to do or act; it signifies to act upon, to produce a change upon. A thing *affects* when it produces any change in our outward circumstances. Whatever *affects* must concern, but what concerns does not always *affect;* for example, the price of corn *affects* the interest of the seller, therefore, it concerns him to keep it up without regard to the public good.

The united powers of hell were bound together for the destruction of mankind, which was *effected* in part. — Addison.

The *effect* is an unfailing index to the amount of the cause. — Whewell.

Patchwork introduced for oratorical *effect.* — J. C. Shairp.

The *effect* was heightened by the wild and lonely nature of the place. — Irving.

To *effect* that which the divine counsel did decree. — Bp. Hurd.

They sailed away without *effecting* their purpose.

The change was *effected* by vinegar. — Boyle.

What he decreed, he *effected.* — Milton.

But this proud man *affects* imperial sway. — Dryden.

The drops of every fluid *affect* a round figure. — Newton.

The climate *affected* their health and spirits. — Macaulay.

Thou dost *affect* my manners. — Shakespeare.

Each of them is *affected* with the beauties of its own kind. — Addison.

Respectfully, Respectively.

Respectfully means in a respectful manner, civilly, courteously. It is often employed as a complimentary closing to letters, notes, invitations, etc.

Respectively means relating to a particular person or thing; belonging to each; particularly. I am yours *respectfully*, I *respectfully* beg to submit this proposition to you.

The impressions from the objects of the senses do mingle *respectively* every one with his kind. — Bacon.

There were four boys, *respectively;* John, James, Henry, and George.

Salary, Wages.

Salary is money paid to a person at regularly fixed intervals for services.

Wages may be also paid at regularly fixed intervals, though when recompense for service is paid at short intervals, as by the day, it is usually called *wages*. *Salary* is also supposed by some to be recompense for services of a higher order; though this last destinction, if it exists, is not always observed.

That they may have their *wages* duly paid them and something over to remember me. — Shakespeare.

The manager drew his *salary* at the end of every month.

Answer, Reply, Rejoinder.

We *answer* a question. We *reply* to an assertion. We make a *rejoinder* to a reply. We *answer* either for the purpose of denying some statement, of giving some information, or contradicting some statement.

We *reply* or *rejoin* to explain or confute.

A *reply* is a response to a formal answer or attack either written or spoken.

A *rejoinder* is a second *reply*, or a *reply* to a *reply* in speech or controversy.

She *answers* him, as if she knew his mind.— Shakespeare.

Do the strings *answer* to thy noble hand. It *answers* the purpose. Old man, who art thou that repliest against God.— Bible.

The temptor stood nor had but to *reply*.— Milton.

The lawyer now proceeded to make his *rejoinder*.

Associate, Companion.

Associates are those who are habitually in our company: *companions* are those who are only occasionally in our company. Our habits are largely formed from our *associates:* Our *companions* do much to add to our happiness. Many persons may be suitable *companions* who would not be fit *associates*.

He succeeded in *associating* his name inseparably with some names which will last as long as our language.— Macaulay.

We see many struggling singly about the world, unhappy for want of an *associate*. — Johnson.

Here are thy sons again ; and I must lose two of the sweetest *companions* in the world. — Shakespeare.

A *companion* is one with whom we share our bread. — Trench.

Business, Occupation.

Business signifies that which makes busy: *occupation* signifies that which takes possession of a person or thing to the exclusion of other things. *Business* is something more urgent and important than *occupation*. A rich man has no occasion to pursue a *business*, but if he is an industrious man he will not be contented without an *occupation*. A person who is busy has a great deal to attend to. Those who are determined by choice to any kind of *business* are indeed more happy than those who are determined by necessity. — Addison.

How little must the ordinary *occupations* of man seem to one who is engaged in so noble a pursuit as the assimulation of himself to the Deity. — Berkley.

Carriage, Gait, Walk.

Carriage as here used signifies the act of carrying the body : *gait* signifies the manner of going : *walk* signifies the manner of walking.

Carriage has reference to the manner in which the body is carried whether in a state of motion or rest, while *gait* has reference to the manner of carrying the limbs and body whenever we move, and *walk* has reference to the manner of carrying the body when we move forward to *walk*.

A person's *carriage* is in some degree natural to him, but may be greatly changed by education. We may contract a certain *gait* by habit. *Walk* is less *definite* than either *carriage* or *gait*.

His gallant *carriage* all the rest did grace.— Stirling.

I do know him by his *gait*.— Shakespeare.

In length of *train* descends her sweeping gown, and by her graceful *walk*, the queen of love is known.

Principal, Principle.

Principal signifies the highest in rank, character, or importance ; that which is considered the most important, as the *principal* officers of the city, the *principal* products of a country, the *principal* men of the town.

Principle signifies a settled rule of action, a fundamental proof or action.

The *principal* men of the town were utterly destitute of *principle*.

We should try rather to be persons of firmly fixed *principles* than to curry favor with *principal* men.

He was chosen *principal* of the school.

Wisdom is the *principal* thing.

The soul of man is an active *principle*.

A good *principle* not rightly understood may prove as hurtful as a bad.

I do not like your *principles*.

Close, Shut.

Close signifies to put together; *shut* signifies to put together so close that no opening is left.

The eyes are *shut* by closing the eyelids; the mouth is *shut* by closing the lips.

Many things are *closed* which cannot be *shut* and many things are *shut* which cannot be closed.

Nothing can be closed except something that consists of more than one part. Nothing can be *shut* except something that has or is supposed to have a cavity. A box is *shut* but it cannot be *closed*. A cut on the hand is *closed*, but it cannot be *shut*.

One frugal supper did our studies *close.*— Dryden.

Shall we be *shut* to that which to the beast is open?— Milton.

Continual, Continued.

What is *continual* may have frequent pauses; what is *continued* goes on without any pause until its termination.

Rains are *continual*. Noises in the street are *continual*. In the frigid zone there is *continued* darkness for the space of five or six months.

He that is of a merry heart hath a *continual* feast.— Prior.

The eye is delighted by a *continual* succession of small landscapes. — Irving.

Our life is one *continued* toil for fame. — Martyn.

By too intense and *continued* application our feeble powers would soon be worn out. — Blair.

Employ, Use.

Employ does not express so much as *use*. We always *use* when we *employ*, but we do not always *employ* when we *use*. We *employ* anything we take into our services for a time. We *use* what we entirely devote to our purpose. Whatever is *employed* by one person may be *employed* by another, or at different times *employed* by the same person, but anything that is *used* is frequently rendered unfit for a similar *use* afterwards. What we *employ* may belong to another person, but what we *use* is supposed to be our exclusive property.

We speak of *employing* persons as well as things, but we speak of *using* things only, and not persons, except in a very degrading sense.

This is a day in which the thoughts ought to be *employed* on serious subjects.— Addison.

Thy vineyard must *employ* the sturdy steer to turn the glebe.— Dryden.

We *employ* certain technical terms in reference to a given subject: We *use* words to express our general meaning.

Some other means I have which may be *used*.— Milton.

Use diligence in business.

Ye valleys low, where the mild whispers *use*
Of shades, and wanton winds, and gushing brooks.
— Milton.

Freedom, Liberty.

Freedom has reference to the simple unsuppressed exercise of our powers, while liberty has reference to previous restraint.

A captive is set at liberty.

The *liberty* of the press, is our great security for *freedom* of thought. A *freedom* may be innocent. A *liberty* does more or less violence to decency. There are little *freedoms* which may be allowed between the youths of different sexes, which will heighten the pleasure of society. A modest woman will resent every *liberty* offered to her as an insult.

" Made captive, yet deserving *freedom* more." — Milton.

" Repeatedly provoked into striking those who had taken *liberties* with him." — Macaulay.

Gross, Total.

Gross implies the whole of anything: that from which nothing has been taken. The *total* includes everything which we wish to include. We may deduct from the *gross* that which does not immediately belong to it. The *total* is that which admits of no deduction. *Gross* also signifies things taken or considered in a large and comprehensive way. Things are said to undergo a *total* change, meaning an entire change.

Hollow, Empty.

Hollow has reference to the body itself. While *empty* refers to foreign bodies. The absence of some of the

materials belonging to a body, constitutes *hollowness.*
The absence of a foreign body constitutes *emptiness.*
What is *empty*, must be *hollow*, but what is *hollow* need
not be *empty.* A hazel nut is *hollow* for the purpose of
receiving the fruit. It is *empty*, when there is no fruit.
If the interior of a tree should rot out, it may become
hollow. If the *hollow* was not filled with some foreign
substance, it would also be empty.

Ingenuous, Ingenious.

Ingenuous means frank, open, and refers to the noble-
ness of character which is inborn. *Ingenious* has reference to the genius or mental powers which are inborn
with life. We love the ingenuous character, on account
of his open and frank disposition, we admire the ingenious man, on account of the endowments of his mind.
A man may confess his faults *ingenuously*, yet defend
them *ingeniously.*

"Being required to explain himself, he ingenuously
confessed."— Ludlow.

"Thus men go wrong with an ingenious skill."

News, Tidings.

News denotes intelligence from any quarter. *Tidings*
denotes expected intelligence from some particular
quarter. *News* is unexpected. *Tidings* are expected.
In time of war everybody is anxious for *news.* Persons
who have relatives in the army, are anxious to have *tidings* from them. We may have no interest in *news*, but
we are always more or less interested in *tidings.* We
may have a curiosity to hear *news*, we have an anxiety to
receive *tidings.*

Novel, New.

Whenever a thing is *novel*, it is always *new*. But it is not every *new* thing that is *novel*.

What is *novel* is usually strange and unexpected; while what is *new*, is ordinarily, usual and expected.

What we have never seen before, or what we have seldom seen, is a *novel* sight. What is seen for the first time is a *new* sight. " We are naturally delighted with *novelty*." — Johnson.

" *New* tribes visit the spacious heavens."— Thomson.

Ray, Beam.

Ray may be used when reference is had to either a large or a small quantity of light. But *beam* is used only when we refer to a large quantity.

We may speak of the *rays* of either the sun, moon, or stars, or any luminous body, but we speak of the *beams* of the sun or the moon.

It is hard to shut a room so that a single *ray* of light will not penetrate its interior.

The lake looks beautiful on a summer's night with the moon *beams* smiling on its waves.

Repose, Recline.

To *repose* signifies to put ourselves in a position which is easy ; while *recline* means to lean back. The man *reposes* on a sofa or in an easy chair ; he may *recline* in a very uncomfortable chair.

Seem, Appear.

Seem signifies to appear like, and is therefore a species of *appear*. Nothing *seems* except that which *appears* in some given form, though anything may *appear*.

Seem is said of that which is in the future, or that which is contingent or doubtful.

Appear is asserted of that which is positive or past.

To say that a thing *appears* to be true, means that the facts as stated go to prove its truthfulness. To say that anything *seems* to be true, means that it has the resemblance of being so, and we infer that it is true.

" A prince of Italy, it *seems*, entertained his mistress on a great lake."— Addison.

" His first principal care being to *appear* unto his people as he would have them be."— Sidney.

Truth, Veracity.

Truth refers to the thing. *Veracity* to the person.

We speak of the *truth* of something that is told, and the *veracity* of the person who told it.

" Whispering tongues can poison *truth.*" — Coleridge.

Some men are to be admired for their *veracity*.

Reality, Truth.

Reality refers to the existence of a thing, while *truth* refers to the report concerning it.

The thing about which a statement is made either is, or is not, a *reality*. The statement made about the thing is either *true* or false.

Writer, Author.

Writer has reference to the act of writing; *author* refers to the act of inventing.

Every *author* may properly be termed a *writer*, but every *writer* is not an *author*.

Compilers and contributors to periodicals are *writers*, but not *authors*.

Poets and historians may be properly termed *authors*.

Custom, Habit.

Custom has reference to things which are done by the majority, while *habit* refers to things done by individuals.

We speak of the *customs* of a nation, and the *habits* of a man.

Custom is the outgrowth of long established practice, and may become a law. There can be no *custom* without usage, but there may be usage without *custom*.

Habits will often arise from *customs*. The custom of attending church may produce habits of piety.

Clothe, Dress.

To *clothe* is to cover the body. To *dress* is to cover it in some particular manner. *Dressing* is a mode of *clothing*. We *clothe* our bodies to protect them from the weather. We *dress* in conformity with some particular custom.

Lucky, Fortunate.

Persons are called *lucky* when they secure something that is wholly unexpected, or when reference is made to something that is purely hazard.

We are spoken of as *fortunate* when we are continually successful in our undertakings.

A *fortunate* man grows rich by successful investments.

A *lucky* man grows rich by securing a prize in a lottery, or some unexpected legacy.

Reason, Cause.

Reasons refer to *actions*, causes to things. *Reasons* are either true or false. *Causes* are either hidden or evident.

A hard wind was the *cause* of the fence blowing down.

It is difficult to give the *reason* for every calculation in trigonometry. A fact is derived from a *cause*. A conclusion is derived from a *reason*.

The hot sun was the *cause* of the butter melting, on top of the man's house; but to discover the *reason* why it was placed there, we must ask the man who owns the house.

Thankful, Grateful.

Thankfulness has reference to the expression of the feelings, while *gratitude* is the feeling itself.

We express our *thanks*, but we look *grateful*.

Gratitude is often too deep to be uttered ; *thankfulness* is uttered. *Thankfulness* is temporary ; *gratitude*, lasting.

Modest, Bashful.

Modest refers to a retiring manner of behavior; *bashfulness* signifies awkwardness of manner.

The *modest* are those who have not too high an opinion of themselves. The *bashful* blush, and hang their heads when spoken to. It is agreeable to converse with the *modest*, but it is painful to converse with the *bashful*.

The *modest* have confidence, but are not conceited. The *bashful* have no self-possession.

EXERCISES IN PRECISION.

The pupil should illustrate, by an original sentence, the precise use of each word in these exercises, he should also, insert the proper word in each blank. The dictionary should be consulted freely.

Abandon, Desert, Forsake.

The brave man will not —— his post in the hour of danger.

I saw a —— village.

I feel almost ——.

Sufficient, Enough.

A greedy man never has —— to eat.

It is —— for you to know that he is alive.

Opportunity, Occasion.

If I should have an —— to call on him, I will improve the —— and present the matter.

I frequently have an —— to go to town.

Conduct, Behavior.

The —— of the firemen was worthy of praise.

The soldiers —— gallantly on the occasion.

Custom, Habit.

Paley has said that man is a bundle of——.

The —— of early rising is very conducive to health.

In many places in Germany it is the —— to dine as early as twelve o'clock.

Duty, Obligation.

It is the —— of parents to attend to the moral training of their children.

I feel myself under many —— to my uncle.

Haste, Hurry.

He ran off in such a —— that I did not get to tell him good-bye.

If you do not make —— you will not get through in time.

Though I am in a great —— I will do it for you.

Manners, Address.

A good —— is not to be acquired by any fixed rules.
His table —— show good breeding.

Remember, Recollect.

I —— perfectly what occurred up to a certain point
of time, but I cannot —— what took place afterwards.

Those whose memories are retentive have but little
difficulty in —— what they have once learned.

Immediate, Instantly.

Admiration is a short lived passion which —— decays
upon growing familiar with its object.

This good news arrived yesterday, and was —— spread
all over town.

Seeing his friend in imminent danger of his life, he
—— went to his rescue.

Hands me, Pretty.

Mr. Jones, the traveler, was a tall —— man.

The forget-me-not is one of the —— flowers I ever
saw.

Saxon ladies have generally —— faces.

Little, Small.

I saw a pretty —— girl standing at the garden gate.

The —— heads do not always belong to the most
stupid persons.

This piece of lead is too —— to weigh much.

Business, Profession.

Manufacturers and bankers carry on a ——.

Clergymen, physicians, etc., follow a ——.

Those who are determined by choice to any particular kind of —— are indeed more happy than those who are determined by necessity.

Genteel, Polite.

A lady of genius will have a —— air about her whole dress.

He is certainly a —— and courteous gentleman.

Mention, Notice.

The great critic I have before ——, though a heathen, has taken —— of the sublime manner in which the law-giver of the Jews has described the creation.

In the course of his conversation he ·—— the badness of the road, and called the attention of his companion to it.

Help, Assist.

It is said that the author was materially —— in his work by a friend.

Had it not been for his uncle who —— him out of his difficulty he would have gone to prison.

I hastened to his —— and soon turned the scale of victory.

Exterior, External.

We should never judge anything by its ——.

A large part of the religion in all countries was found to consist of —— ceremonies.

Great, Big.

The sack will not be —— enough to hold all that we wish to put into it.

The —— the difficulty, the harder we should strive to overcome it.

This hat is not —— enough for him.

Strong, Robust.

He had a —— constitution.

Three —— men could scarcely hold him down.

Those who are physically —— are sometimes weak in mind.

The huntsmen are gay, —— and bold.

Ability, Capacity.

It is never necessary to explain a thing twice to a pupil of good ——.

Few persons exercise their —— to the utmost.

The —— and prudence of the general is all that saved the army.

Value, Worth.

The —— of the book can hardly be estimated.

How much is that book —— ?

The —— of a man's estate has nothing to do with his moral ——.

Invent, Discover.

Some one said that printing was the most important —— of modern times.

The Chinese had —— the attractive power of the load-stone from remotest antiquity.

Native, Natural.

In heaven we shall pass from the darkness of our —— ignorance into the broad light.

Scripture ought to be understood according to the familiar —— way of construction.

Lay, Lie.

A fragrant shower of rain had —— the dust.

He has been —— down about two hours.

He intends to —— in a supply of wood for the winter.

Trust, Credit.

Though it seems plausible, we attach but little —— to the report.

We can put no —— in a liar nor give no —— to his tales.

Vacant, Empty.

A —— hour wants filling up.

An —— title has nothing in it.

When you speak he listens with a —— eye.

Pleasure, Happiness.

Wealth though it assists our —— cannot procure us —— .

The fragrance of flowers gives us —— .

Hear, Listen.

If you —— to a conversation, you may —— many improving remarks.

There is an old proverb : —— never —— any good of themselves.

We —— attentively but —— nothing more.

INDEX.